The ENORMOUS BOOK OF HOT JOKES for kool kiDS

The ABC 'Wave' device is a trademark of the
Australian Broadcasting Corporation and is used
under licence by HarperCollins*Publishers* Australia.

This edition first published in 2004 by ABC Books for
the Australian Broadcasting Corporation.
Reprinted by HarperCollins*Publishers* Australia Pty Limited
ABN 36 009 913 517
harpercollins.com.au

HarperCollins*Publishers*
Level 13, 201 Elizabeth Street, Sydney, NSW 2000, Australia
31 View Road, Glenfield, Auckland 0627, New Zealand
A 53, Sector 57 Noida, UP, India
77–85 Fulham Palace Road, London W6 8JB, United Kingdom
2 Bloor Street East, 20th floor, Toronto, Ontario M4W 1A8, Canada
10 East 53rd Street, New York NY 10022, USA

National Library of Australia Cataloguing-in-publication data:

The enormous book of hot jokes for kool kids.
Children aged 6–12 years.
ISBN 978 0 7333 1405 6.
1. Wit and humor, Juvenile. I. Jones, Andy, 1961 – .
II. Australian Broadcasting Corporation.
A828.02

Cover design by Pigs Might Fly
Illustrated by Mike Spoor and Stephen Axelsen
Files by Midland Typesetters, Maryborough, Victoria
Printed and bound in Australia by Griffin Press
70gsm Classic used by HarperCollins*Publishers* is a natural, recyclable product made
from wood grown in sustainable forests. The manufacturing processes conform to
the environmental regulations in the country of origin, Finland.

11   13

The ENORMOUS BOOK OF HOT JOKES for kool kids

COMPILED BY
Andy Jones

ILLUSTRATED BY
Mike Spoor and Stephen Axelsen

ABC
Books

ACKNOWLEDGEMENTS

Thanks to children all over Australia for their lively imaginations and for their endless enthusiasm for joke telling. Special thanks to the children and staff of the following schools:

Allanson PS
Allenswood PS
Armidale City Public School
Ashford Central School
Augusta PS
Australind PS
Baan Baa Public School
Bayldon PS
Beachlands PS
Beauty Point PS
Beecroft PS
Bell Post PS
Bellata PS
Bellbird Public School
Bermagui PS
Bethany College Kogarah
Beverley DHS
Boyanup PS
Boyup Brook DHS
Bridgetown Primary School and Lisa Field
Busselton West PS
Cloverdale PS
Collie Catholic College
Dandaragan PS
Darkan DHS
Dunsborough PS
Flinders Park PS
Gingin DHS
Greenock PS

Katanning PS
Korakonui School
Kyeemagh PS
Mandurah North PS
Merredin North PS
Merredin South PS
Moora PS
Morawa DHS
Narromine PS
Narrogin PS
Our Lady of the River School
Parramatta PS
Pemberton DHS
Petersham Kindergarten
Petersham PS
Port Kennedy PS
Rostrata PS
Sacred Heart PS, Ulverstone
Seaforth PS
Singleton PS
Tailem Bend PS
Taverners Hill PS
The Entrance PS
Vasse PS
Victoria Park PS
Wilson Park PS
Woodanilling PS
York DHS

CONTENTS

It's Raining Cats and Dogs

**It's raining cats and dogs tonight
And there ain't no poodle within sight
Watch a dog that likes to tick
Wind him up to do a trick ...**

Q What sort of dog can tell the time?
A A watch dog.

Kate G., aged 7

Q Why did the dog wear a watch?
A Because he wanted to be a watch dog.

Ashi W., aged 7

Q What did one flea say to the other flea?
A Shall we walk or take the dog?

Emma M., aged 7

Q What did the cat have for breakfast?

A Mice Bubbles.

Abbie S., aged 8

Q What do you get when you cross a cocker spaniel with a rooster?

A A cockerpoodledoo.

Merey T., aged 10

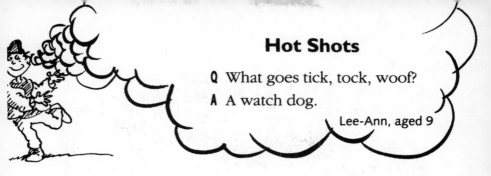

Hot Shots

Q What goes tick, tock, woof?
A A watch dog.

Lee-Ann, aged 9

Two dogs started fighting outside a milkbar. The shop-keeper yelled at the dogs but they kept on fighting. Just then a boy walked up to the dogs and put his feet between them. The dogs became very quiet and fell asleep.

'How did you do that?' the shopkeeper asked. 'I've got Hush Puppies on,' replied the boy.

Kristie B., aged 11

Q What do you get if you cross a cat with a pillow?
A A caterpillar.

Susie M., aged 10

Flying and Floating

Fish can swim
Bees can fly
Birds drop messages
From the sky ...

Q Why isn't there much honey in Brazil?

A Because there's only one 'B' in Brazil.   Nicole J., aged 9

Q What do you get if you cross an Australian bird with a rabbit's home?

A A kookaburrow.   Rodney U., aged 11

Q What goes zzub, zzub?

A A bee flying backwards.   Lee B., aged 10

Q What happens when ducks fly upside down?

A They quack up.   Lee-Anne, aged 8

Q What does a bee look for when it crosses its legs?

A A BP station.   Joel M., aged 6

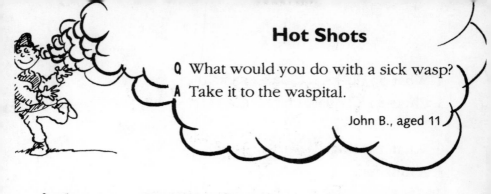

Hot Shots

Q What would you do with a sick wasp?
A Take it to the waspital.

John B., aged 11

Q There were two birds sitting on a wire, one named Pete and the other named Repeat. If Pete flies away, who is left?
A Repeat.
... There were two birds ... ✓

Jason J., aged 7

Q What sea monster sounds like a huge monster's money?
A A giant squid. ✓

Phillipa, aged 8

Q Why do bees hum?
A Because they always forget the words.

Katrina Ann B., aged 8

Q What is black and white and dangerous?
A A magpie with a machine gun. ✓ Casey M., aged 10

Q What do ducks eat for a snack?
A Cheese and quackers!

Ryan W., aged 7

Q What fish sings?
A A tuna fish.

Tanya T., aged 11

Q What did the bee say to the flower?
A Hi, honey.

Hani M., aged 7

Q What do fish play on the piano?
A Scales!

Vicky S., aged 9

Q What's a duck's favourite TV show?
A The feather forecast.

Belinda F., aged 11

Q What is yellow and dangerous?
A Shark infested custard.

Gareth H., aged 9

Hot Shots

Q What says 'Quick! Quick!'?
A A duck with hiccups.

Belinda F., aged 11

Q Why is a flower like the letter 'A'?
A Because a bee always comes after it.   Cherylyn N., aged 6

Q What did one bee say to the other bee?
A Your honey or your life!   Skye M., aged 7

Q Where would you weigh a whale?
A At a whaleweigh station.   Elody D., aged 10

Q What did the boy octopus say to the girl octopus?
A I want to hold your hand hand hand hand hand hand
hand hand. ✓   Melanie C., aged 10

Q Why are fish so smart?
A Because they swim around in schools.   Emma G., aged 10

Q What do you get when you cross a bumble bee with
a rabbit?
A A honey bunny.   Mitchell D., aged 6

A Hop, Squeak

and a Jump

A woolly jumpered kangaroo
And two white rabbits skating through
Collide outback with such a thump –
Sounds like a hop, squeak and a jump ...

Q What do you call a rabbit with fleas?

A Bugs bunny.   Rachel D., aged 11

Q Why did Mickey Mouse catch a rocket into space?

A Because he wanted to find Pluto.   Carinne C., aged 8

Q What's white with long ears, whiskers and sixteen wheels?

A Two white rabbits on roller skates.   Mitchell D., aged 6

Hot Shots

Q What kind of boots do koalas wear?
A Gum boots.   Melanie C., aged 10

Q What do you get when you cross a kangaroo with a sheep?
A A woolly jumper. ✓   Alison H., aged 8

Q What do you get when you pour boiling water down a rabbit hole?
A Hot cross bunnies. ✓   Jessica and Ann O., aged 6 and 4

Q What did one mouse do when the other fell in the river.
A Applied mouse-to-mouse resuscitation.   Greg K., aged 8

Q What kind of rabbit can jump higher than a house?
A Any kind of rabbit because houses can't jump. ✓
                    Krystal M., aged 7

Q What game do bunnies like best?
A Hopscotch.   Aaron C., aged 10

Elephants

They amble along like great steamrollers
Watch out for their tusks – oh holy molars!
Beware the fence that's in their path –
The strawberry patch will make you laugh ...

Q How do you get down off an elephant?
A You don't get down off an elephant, you get down
off a duck.   Tobi J., aged 8

Q If there were two elephants under one umbrella, why
didn't they get wet?
A It wasn't raining.   Luana H., aged 6

Q How do you keep an
elephant from charging?
A Take away its credit card.
Cynthia, aged 11

Hot Shots

Q What is as big as an elephant but weighs nothing at all?

A The shadow of an elephant.

Kathleen, aged 6

Q Why did the elephant paint his toenails rainbow colours?

A So he could hide in a Smartie box.

Simon P., aged 10

Q What do you get if you cross an elephant and a kangaroo?

A Holes all over Australia.

Alisha, aged 10

Q How can you hide an elephant in a strawberry patch?

A Paint its toenails red.

Katrina Ann B., aged 8

Q What do elephants have that no other animals have?

A Baby elephants.

Candice D., aged 10

Q What time is it when an elephant sits on a fence?

A Time to get a new one. ✓

Carolyn M., aged 8

Far Flung and

Foreign

From exotic locations and far off lands;
The darkest jungles and desert sands;
From polar caps to the tallest trees
Foreign animals, if you please ...

Q What do you get if you cross a kangaroo with a year?
A A leap year.   Alana L., aged 7

Q Why did the monkey put a chop on top of his head?
A Because he thought he was a griller.   Jennie B., aged 8

Q What do you call a monkey with bananas in his ears?
A Anything you like – he can't hear you. ✓   Nicole F., aged 7

Q Why does a stork stand on one foot?
A Because if it didn't, it would fall over.   Belinda F., aged 11

Q How can you catch a squirrel in your garden?
A Climb up a tree and act like a nut.   Alison R., aged 8

Q What's black and white and red all over?
A A sunburnt penguin.   Nikki S., aged 9

Hot Shots

Q What do you get if you cross a giraffe with a porcupine?

A A three metre toothbrush.

Colin B., aged 9

Q What animals can jump higher than the Sydney Harbour Bridge?

A All animals can, as the Sydney Harbour Bridge can't jump. ✔

Emma G., aged 8

Q What's black and white and has wheels?

A A zebra with roller skates.

Linda, aged 10

Q What's big, red and eats rocks?

A A big, red rock eater. ✔

Anthony S., aged 7

Q Why does a dinosaur have such a long neck?

A So that he can keep away from his smelly feet.

Dylan, aged 6

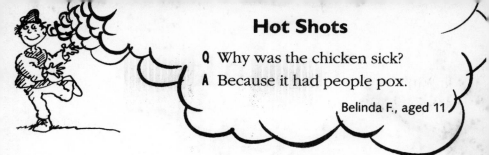

Hot Shots

Q Why was the chicken sick?
A Because it had people pox.

Belinda F., aged 11

Q What's black and white and red all over?
A A skunk with nappy rash. ✓

Melissa H., aged 8

Q What is the first thing a little ape learns in school?
A The Ape, B, C.

Candice D., aged 10

Q What is big, white and furry and found in outback Australia?
A A lost polar bear. ✓

Nicole Louise K., aged 9

Q What has two humps and lives in Alaska?
A A lost camel.

Katrina Ann B., aged 8

Q What did the lion say when he saw some kids on rollerblades?
A Yum, yum! Meals on wheels. ✓

Sathyar Joy D., aged 7

Q What do you call bears without ears?
A 'b'.

Benjamin H., aged 7

Funky

Farmyard

Pigs that know karate
Give a mighty pork chop;
Sheep all go for hair cuts
At the baa-baa shop.
Cows go to the moo-vies and read The Daily Moos;
Bulls that charge for everything are certain to amuse ...

Q What do you get if you cross a hen and a waiter?

A A hen that lays tables. Kate, aged 6

Q What shoes do chickens wear?

A Reebok-bok-bok-bok-bok-bok ... Kerry S., aged 10

Q What's a horse's favourite game?

A Stable tennis. Tonya M., aged 9

Q How do you stop a pig from smelling?

A Put a clothes peg on its nose. Lisa L., aged 12

Q Why do horses only wear shoes?

A Because they'd look silly in socks.

Emily M., aged 10

Hot Shots

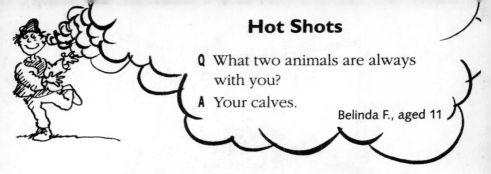

Q What two animals are always with you?

A Your calves.

Belinda F., aged 11

Q Which is better – a cow or a bull?

A A cow because the cow gives milk but a bull always charges.

Benjamin G., aged 9

Q What newspaper do cows read?

A The Daily Moos.

Katrina Ann B., aged 8

Q Where do cows go on dates?
A To the moo-vies.

Sathyar Joy D., aged 7

Q Why is it hard to talk with a goat around?
A Because goats always butt in.

Susie M., aged 10

Q What do you call a bull when it is asleep?
A A bulldozer.

Ben T., aged 6

Q What do you get from a pig who knows karate?
A A pork chop.

Alisha M., aged 9

Hot Shots

Q What do you get if you cross a cow with a blender?
A A milk shake.

Daniel T., aged 9

Q What do you call a lamb with a machine gun?
A Lambo. ✓
Q What do you call its father?
A Rambo. ✓

Brock M., aged 9

Q What do you get if you cross a lamb and a dog?
A A lamb-rover.

Alex, aged 6

Q Where do sheep go to get their hair cut?
A To the baa-baa shop.

Andrew M., aged 9

They're Odd,

They're Weird
They're Kinda Strange

**Everyone's mad in their own special way,
We're all individual with the things that we say.
To some it's eccentric, to others it's hip,
Making friends is like picking from a lucky dip ...**

Q What do you call a wicked old woman who lives by
the sea?

A A sandwich.

Melanie C., aged 10

Q What do you call a man in the ocean with no arms and no legs?

A Bob.

Luke E., aged 11

Q Why did the man take a pencil to bed with him?

A So he could draw the curtains.

Steven M., aged 11

Q Why did Granny put wheels on her rocking chair?

A She wanted to rock and roll.

Rachel D., aged 11

Q What did the alien say to the petrol pump?

A Why have you got your finger stuck in your ear?

Tarryn C., aged 7

Q How can you make a tall man short?

A Borrow $50 from him.

Belinda F., aged 11

Q What did the kid say when he saw someone pulled in by a huge fan?

A Ha, ha! Sucked in.

Mark F., aged 10

Q What kind of person is fed up with people?
A A cannibal.

Rodney U., aged 11

Q What did the constipated mathematician do?
A Worked it out with a pencil.

Gemma W., aged 11

Karl K., aged 11

Q What did the doctor say when an invisible man tried to make an appointment ?
A Sorry. I can't see him now. ✓

Katharine S., aged 7

Hot Shots

Q Why did the girl take a ladder to school?

A Because she went to high school.

Shane M., aged 10

Q What happened to the man who stole a calendar?

A He got twelve months.

Rodney U., aged 11

Q Who was the first man underwater?

A James Pond. ✓

Rodney U., aged 11

Q Why was screaming coming from the kitchen?

A Because the cook was beating the eggs and whipping the cream. ✓

Craig S., aged 8

Q What do you do if your toe drops off in the middle of the road?

A Call a toe truck.

Aaron C., aged 10

33

A lady walked into a shoe store and asked for a pair of alligator shoes. 'Of course,' said the owner. 'What size are your alligator's feet?'

Rebecca C., aged 11

Q Why did the man in gaol catch chicken pox?
A He wanted to break out.

Tim C., aged 7

WHY DID YOU SWALLOW 60 CENTS?

IT WAS MY LUNCH MONEY

A man and a woman were walking through the jungle when suddenly a lion pounced upon them, half swallowing the lady.

'Shoot! Shoot!' cried the woman.

'I can't ,' replied the man. 'There's no film left!'

Lisa L., aged 12

Q What goes he ha bonk?

A A man laughing his head off.

Jessica A., aged 9

Q If Batman and Robin were run over by a steamroller, what would they be called?

A Flatman and Ribbon. ✓   Belinda F., aged 11

Q Why did the man have to repair the horn of his car?

A Because it didn't give a hoot.   Serin A., aged 11

Q What do you call a lady standing in the middle of a tennis court?

A Annette.   Lucia G., aged 7

Q Adam and Eve and Pinchme went to a lake. Adam and Eve drowned. Who is left?

A Pinchme!   Bronwyn H., aged 12

Q Why did the robber have a bath?

A To make a clean getaway. ✓   Teresa C., aged 9

Q How do you get a one-armed Australian out of a tree?
A Wave to him.   Teresa C., aged 9

Q Why did the lady fall out her window?
A Because she was ironing her curtains.   Richard F., aged 9

Q How do you fit one hundred people in a car?
A Pick up 99 and Maxwell Smart.   Rainie H., aged 9

Q How can you tell that cemeteries are popular?
A Because people are dying to get in.   Belinda F., aged 11

Bug Off

Slime Bag!

**They creep and crawl and slither along,
Insects and bugs and snakes sooooo long;
Multiple legs and hungry dispositions,
You'll find them in peculiar positions ...**

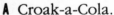

Q What's green and goes red at the flick of a switch?

A A frog in a blender.   John B., aged 11

Q Where do tadpoles change into frogs?

A In the croak room.   Emma G., aged 10

Q What's a frog's favourite drink?

A Croak-a-Cola.   Maria K., aged 10

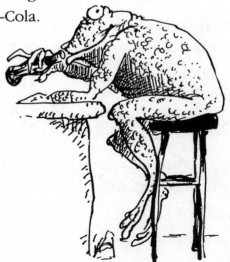

Hot Shots

Q What's the first thing a little snake learns in school?

A Hiss-tory.

Candice D., aged 10

Q What kind of grass jumps?

A A grasshopper.

Lena I., aged 8

Q What has fifty legs and cannot walk?

A Half a centipede.

Rodney U., aged 11

Q How do you start a flea race?

A Say one-two-flea go!

Emma M., aged 7

Q I have fifteen eyes, eight noses, four mouths, eighteen legs and fifteen arms. What am I?

A Very ugly.

Emma W., aged 11

Q What is a caterpillar?

A A rich worm in a fur coat.

Serin A., aged 11

39

Q How do you tell one end of a worm from the other?

A Tickle him in the middle and see which end laughs.

Angus C., aged 9

Q What did the boy snake say to the girl snake?

A Give me a hiss.

Melissa C., aged 9

Q Why was the mother flea so sad?

A Her children were going to the dogs.

Emma T., aged 11

Q What does a caterpillar do on New Year's Day?

A Turns over a new leaf.

Nicole A., aged 7

40

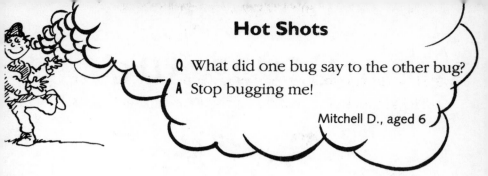

Hot Shots

Q What did one bug say to the other bug?
A Stop bugging me!

Mitchell D., aged 6

Q Why can't a ladybird ever hide?
A Because it is always spotted.

Skye M., aged 7

Q What is an insect's favourite band?
A The Beatles.

Monique T., aged 10

Q What's worse than a worm in your pear?
A Half a worm.

Vanessa L., aged 7

Gross and Grotty

**The
Grottiest,
Yukkiest,
Smelliest
Ickiest
most disgustingest
jokes
for the cleanest kids ...**

Can I tell you a real dirty joke?
The man fell in the mud.   Daniel, aged 6

Now for a clean joke.
He had a wash.   Daniel, aged 6

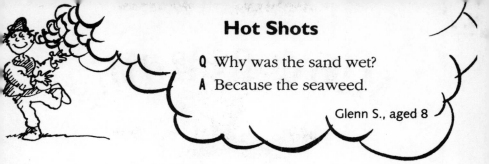

Hot Shots

Q Why was the sand wet?
A Because the seaweed.

Glenn S., aged 8

Q How do you make a hankie dance?
A Put a bit of boogie in it.   Jackson P., aged 11

Q Have you heard the one about the garbage truck?
A Don't worry, it's just a load of rubbish.   Megan R., aged 11

Q What did the floor say to the desk?
A I can see your drawers?   Penny K., aged 10

Q Why was the sea bed unhappy?
A Well, you'd be unhappy if you had crabs on your
bottom.   Naomi S., aged 9

Q What do you get up a clean nose?
A Finger prints.   Debra D., aged 8

Q What goes 250 kilometres per hour down a human
nose?
A A Lambourgreenie.   Alex P., aged 10

Mind Bending

Brain Stretching

Stretch that mind and bend that brain
Sometimes thinking causes pain
Don't despair your brain is smart
All it needs is a stretching start ...

Q What is a naval destroyer?
A A hoola-hoop with a nail in it.

Angus G., aged 11

Q What is round and nasty?
A A vicious circle.

Michael S., aged 11

Q What did the Nepalese farmer say when his rooster laid an egg?
A Himalayer.

Leisa C., aged 10

Q Why did the golfer take two pairs of trousers to the golf course?
A In case he got a hole in one.

Rainie H., aged 9

Hot Shots

Q Why do basketballers need a hankie?
A Because they dribble a lot.

Madeline M., aged 10

Q What did the Olympic sneezing champion win?
A A cold medal.

Michael M., aged 9

Q Why have you got a fried egg on your head, Syd?
A Because a boiled egg rolls off.

Belinda F., aged 11

Q What is a Lapplander?
A A clumsy man on a bus.

Belinda F., aged 11

Q What do you call a one-eyed monster on a bike?
A A cycle-ops.

Leigh S., aged 7

Q Why did the pig run away from the sty?
A Because he thought all the other pigs were taking him for grunted.

Leigh S., aged 7

Who's Got

the Guts?

**Ghosts have no body, skeletons no guts,
One-handed monsters have a feather light touch;
Ghouls that drool and go bump in the night,
Don't be frightened, just turn on the light ...**

Q Why wouldn't the skeleton jump off the cliff?
A He didn't have the guts to.   David B., aged 7

Q How did Frankenstein eat his dinner?
A He bolted it.   Phillipa, aged 8

Q What do ghosts eat for dinner?
A Spook-etti.   Daniel F., aged 7

Hot Shots

Q What do you get if you leave bones out in the sun?

A A skeletan.

Daniel F., aged 7

Q Why couldn't the skeleton go to the ball?

A Because it had nobody to dance with.

Tom J., aged 7

Q Do ghosts take showers?

A No. They take Boo-ble baths.

Andrew M., aged 9

Q Why should skeletons never wear shorts?

A They have boney knees.

Andrew M., aged 9

Q Why is a ghost like a cold breeze?

A Because it makes people shiver.

Andrew M., aged 9

Q Why didn't the ghost go out after work?

A He was dead tired.

Andrew M., aged 9

47

Q Do zombies have trouble getting dates?

A No. They usually manage to dig someone up. Anonymous

Q What's a ghost's favourite party game?

A Haunt and seek.   Aaron S., aged 10

Q What do witches wear on their hair?

A Scare spray.   Cynthia, aged 11

Q What does a boy monster do when a girl monster rolls her eyes at him?

A He picks them up and rolls them back to her.
                                                           Sarah T., aged 8

Q What do you call a monster sleeping in a chandelier?

A A light sleeper.   Janice, aged 10

Q How do monsters unlock their front doors?

A With skeleton keys.   Anonymous

Hot Shots

Q What did the skeleton say to his girlfriend?

A I love every bone in your body.

Suleyman D., aged 10

Q Why did the little vampires stay up all night?

A Because they were studying for a blood test.

Shorna S., aged 10

Q What did the Mother Ghost say to the Baby Ghost when they got into the car?

A Fasten, your sheet belt.

Brooke F., aged 9

Q Why did the monster baseball game end early?

A Someone dropped the bat and it flew away.   Anonymous

Q What's a skeleton?

A A person with their outsides off and their insides out.

Pamela D., aged 10

Q What do you call a four headed monster that weighs twenty tonnes?

A Sir.   Ian W., aged 7

Q Why did the one-handed monster cross the road?

A To get to the second-hand shop.

Mario G., aged 10

49

What!

What is one way to start off a question
All the what questions are too numerous to mention.
Like 'What goes green at the thought of detention?'
What can be your own invention ...

Q What did the doctor say to the chimney?

A Smoking is bad for you.

Damien, aged 10

Q What has four wheels and flies?

A A garbage truck.

Irene S., aged 8

Q What is rhubarb?

A Celery with high blood pressure.

Angus G., aged 7

Q What is something that can't walk but can run?

A A river.

Chris S., aged 10

Q What do you get when a fishing rod catches on fire?

A A hot rod.

Damien, aged 10

50

Hot Shots

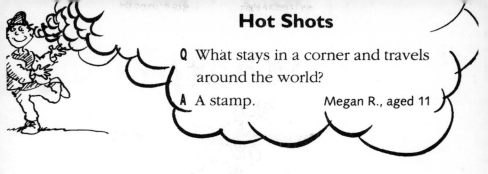

Q What stays in a corner and travels around the world?
A A stamp. Megan R., aged 11

Q What do you call a boy with headphones on?
A Anything you like. He can't hear you. Haig C., aged 10

Q What did the red ribbon say to the green ribbon?
A Why don't you and I tie the knot. Lisa S., aged 9

Q What kind of shoes don't go on your feet.
A Tissues. Cynthia, aged 7

Q What did the father belt say to the baby belt?
A Buckle up, son. Christopher G., aged 7

Q What has two hands, but no fingers?
A A clock. Melinda, aged 8

Q What do you write on a car's grave?
A Rust in peace. Tom P., aged 10

How Now

How could so many? How did so few?
How could he know? How could she too?
How does it go? How does it stop?
How can it be? How can it not?

Q How did the rocket loose his job?
A He was fired.

Cynthia, aged 11

Q How do you make a jacket last?
A Make the trousers first.

Angus G.

Q How do you cut the sea in half?
A With a sea saw.

Dean I., aged 10

Q How did the man mow the lawn?
A With a lawn-mower, of course!!

Kellie, aged 8

Q How do you start a teddy bear race?
A Say 'Ready, teddy, go!'

Jennifer A., aged 6

Oh My,

Tell Me Why

Why does a flower attract a bee?
Why does 'd' come after 'c'?
Why does jelly wobble on its own?
Why is there a ring in a telephone ...

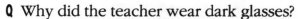

Q Why did Polly put the kettle on?
A Because she didn't
have anything else to wear.   Evan G.

Q Why did the teacher wear dark glasses?
A Because she had such a bright class.   Evan G.

Q Why are Saturday and Sunday strong days?
A Because the others are weekdays.   Evan G.

Q Why can't a bike stand up?
A It's two tyred.   Amy H., aged 10

Q Why was Cinderella hopeless at sport?
A Because she had a pumpkin for a coach.   Jordan W., aged 5

Tasty, Tasty,

Tasty!

There's sultanas and prunes but I can't find a date;
The mayonnaise is dressing, trying not to be late;
The salad is screaming 'Hey lettuce, come in!'
The biscuit can't be found because it's wafer thin ...

Q What did the mayonnaise say to the fridge?

A Close the door, I'm dressing.   Kellie, aged 8

Q Why don't people eat money?

A Because it's too rich.   Lauren M., aged 7

Q What did the baby corn say to the mother corn?

A Where's pop corn?   Glenn S., aged 8

Q What has one horn and gives milk?

A A milk truck.   Jedda T., aged 9

Hot Shots

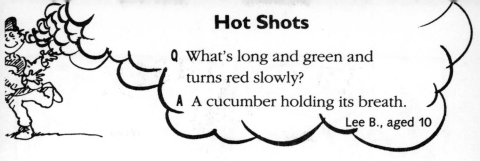

Q What's long and green and turns red slowly?

A A cucumber holding its breath.

Lee B., aged 10

Q What train eats chewing gum?

A A choo choo train.

Melinda , aged 10

Q Why did the sultana go out with the prune?

A Because it couldn't find a date.

Melinda , aged 10

Q How do you drop a pizza ten metres without breaking it?

A Drop it eleven metres and it will stay intact for the first ten metres.

Barry S., aged 9

Q Why did the biscuit cry?

A Because his mother was a wafer so long.

Miss W.

Q Why did the jelly wobble?

A Because it saw the apple turnover.　　　Andrew P., aged 11

Q Why did the tomato blush?

A Because he saw the salad dressing.　　　Naomi S., aged 9

Q Why did the jellybean jump in the water?

A Because he wanted to be a lifesaver.　　　Kellie, aged 8

Drrrrrrr ...

Corny!

Errrrr ... states a fact of the yukky kind;
Furrrr ... is the stuff on a camel's behind;
Herrrr ... is a bounding bunny thing ya know;
Drrrrr ... sums it up from woe to go ...

Q What starts with *t*, ends with *t* and has *t* inside it?
A A teapot.

Emily W., aged 6

Have you heard the joke about the highest wall in the world?
I better not tell you – you might not get over it.

Jaimi B., aged 6

I'd better not tell you the joke about butter – you might spread it!

Danielle S., aged 10

Patient: Doctor, Doctor! I think I'm shrinking!
Doctor: Well, you'll just have to be a little patient.

Melissa C., aged 9

Q What did the clothes line say to the shirt?
A You'll hang for this.

Alisha M., aged 9

Fred: Did you like the story about the dog who ran two miles to fetch a stick?

Jeff: No, I thought it was too far-fetched. Robert I., aged 10

Q What do you say to a wave?
A Nothing. Just wave back. Jason L., aged 10

Q What is the last thing you take off before you go to bed?
A Your feet off the floor. Jason L., aged 10

Q Who is the strongest man in the world?
A A policeman because he can hold up the traffic with one hand. Tim F., aged 9

Q What do you call a doll with a chop and sausage on its back?
A A Barbie. Vanessa F., aged 7

Q What happens if you drop a red hat in a blue sea?
A It gets wet.

David H., aged 7

Hot Shots

Q What did the stamp say to the envelope?
A I guess I'm stuck on you.

Alisha M., aged 9

Q Did you take a bath today?
A Why, was there one missing.

Kristy M., aged 9

Q What did the man say to the germ?
A You make me sick!

Alisha M., aged 9

Q What did the water say to the sea?
A Let's make waves.

James E., aged 7

Q What is green, has eight legs and would kill you if it fell on you from out of a tree?
A A billiard table.

Anonymous

Q Where do we get our air from?
A From the airport.

Pauline E., aged 9

Q What can you serve but not eat?
A A tennis ball.   Belinda F., aged 11

Q What would you get if you dialled
49783446723557463392837462?
A A blister on your finger.   Ryan G., aged 9

Q What do you get when you step on a grape?
A A little wine.   Timothy S., aged 7

Q What is a good cure for a runny nose?
A A tap on the head.   Tony R., aged 6

Q What is always behind time?
A The back of a clock.
                                    Sheree O., aged 9

Q What did the digital clock say to its mother?
A Look, Mum! No hands.   Sheree O., aged 9

Q Why didn't the man die when he drank poison?
A Because he was in the living room.   Yazmin S., aged 9

Radical Road
Crossing

**Really radical road rules
For chickens with lots of heart;
Sometimes all they need to cross
Is a gentle push to start ...**

Q Why did the turtle cross the road?
A To go to the Shell Station.   Carmen, aged 8

Q Why did the orange stop in the middle of the road?
A Because it wanted to play squash.   Samantha G., aged 8

Q Why did the chicken cross the road?
A To prove that he wasn't a chicken.   Martin M., aged 8

Q Why did the computer cross the road?
A Because it was programmed by the chicken.

Claire D., aged 11

Q Why did the pig stop in the middle of the road?
A Because the butcher was at the other side.

Andrew S., aged 8

Q Why did the punk cross the road?
A Because the chicken was nailed to his head.

Jillian C., aged 10

Q Why did the dinosaur cross the road?
A Because the chicken wasn't invented.

Carmen, aged 8

Q Why did the grubby rabbit cross the road twice?
A He was a dirty double-crosser.

Melanie C., aged 10

Q Why did the orange stop in the middle of the road?
A Because it ran out of juice.

Catherine L., aged 9

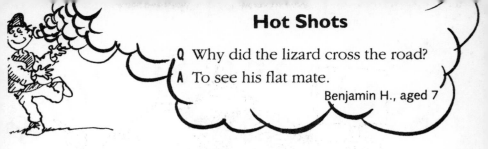

Hot Shots

Q Why did the lizard cross the road?
A To see his flat mate.

Benjamin H., aged 7

Q Why did the chicken cross the road?
A Because he saw a chick.

Sarah P., aged 9

Q Why did the chicken stop at the side of the road?
A Because he had bubble gum stuck to his feet.

Stacey P., aged 10

Q Why did the bubble gum cross the road?
A It was stuck to the chicken's foot.

Michelle D., aged 10

Words and Spelling
Take Some Telling

**Rs that roll and Ps that pop
Make words that sound like rollipop!
Ds that ding and Is that ing
Help make words like dingaling ...**

Q What happened to the boy on Cannibal Island?
A He was ate before he was seven.

Leigh S., aged 7

Q Can February march?
A No, but April may.

Kristie B., aged 11

Q Why are there only 18 letters in the alphabet?
A Because ET went home in a UFO and the CIA went after him.

Gemma W., aged 11

Q What is the laziest letter in the alphabet?
A E, because, it's always in bed.

Philip B., aged 7

Q What's the difference between a lion with a toothache and a rainy day?
A One roars with pain and the other pours with rain.

Tami P., aged 9

Hot Shots

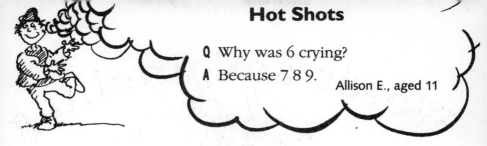

Q Why was 6 crying?
A Because 7 8 9.

Allison E., aged 11

Q Who invented fractions?
A Henry the eighth.

Cynthia, aged 8

Q Spell mouse trap with three letters?
A C – A – T.

Elena Z., aged 9

Q What ten-letter word starts with gas?
A A-U-T-O-M-O-B-I-L-E

Elena Z., aged 9

Q When does Thursday come before Wednesday?
A In a dictionary.

Kelly E., aged 11

Q How do you make varnish disappear?
A Take out the *r*.

Anne-Marie H., aged 10

Knock, Knock ...

Knock-knock who's there? Who could it be?
Knock-knock who's there? Still who? Still me!
Knock-knock who's there? Arch who? Bless me!
Knock-knock who's there? Open up and see ...

Knock, knock.
Who's there?
Boo.
Boo who?
Don't cry, it's only a joke.

Penny L.

Knock, knock
Who's there?
Letter who?
Let her in or she'll knock
the door down.

Christine H., aged 8

Knock, knock
Who's there?
Oscar.
Oscar who?
Oscar silly question and
you get a silly answer.

Philip B., aged 7

Hot Shots

Knock, knock!
Who's there?
Have you forgotten
me already?   Adam, aged 6

Knock, knock!
Who's there?
Bear.
Bear who?
Bear bum.
                Joshua, aged 6

Knock, knock!
Who's there?
Tuba.
Tuba who?
Tuba toothpaste.
                Kristopher, aged 6

Knock, knock!
Who's there?
Phyllis.
Phyllis who?
Fill us a glass of water.
                Claire, aged 6

Knock, knock!
Who's there?
Good.
Good who?
Goodnight.
                Brendon, aged 7

Knock, knock!
Who's there?
Cows go.
Cows go who?
No, cows go moo.
                Rachael, aged 7

Knock, knock.
Who's there?
Still.
Still who?
Still knocking.
                Megan, aged 6

Knock, knock.
Who's there?
Arch.
Arch who.
Bless you!
                Rebecca S., aged 9

Knock, knock!
Who's there?
Amos.
Amos who?
A mosquito.
                Matthew, aged 7

House-holed Humour

**A house is a home whether burrow or nest,
A place to put your feet up and have a rest;
Where corners meet walls and fences surround,
Where windows can look and stories abound ...**

Q What happened to the wooden car with the wooden engine and wooden wheels?

A It wooden go.

Lucy A., aged 8

Q What did the old phone say to the young phone?

A You're too young to get engaged.

Lisa W., aged 9

Q What invention allows you to see through walls?

A A window.

Michael S., aged 8

Hot Shots

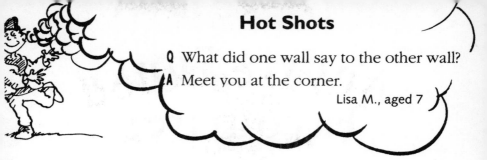

Q What did one wall say to the other wall?

A Meet you at the corner.

Lisa M., aged 7

Q What did the traffic light say to the car?

A Don't look now, I'm changing.

Guy B., aged 8

Q What did the big chimney say to the little chimney?

A You're too young to smoke.

Belinda J., aged 8

Q What is an Ig?

A An eskimo's house without a toilet.

Naomi S., aged 9

Q What did the fence say to the house?

A I've got you surrounded.

Ashleigh W., aged 7

Q What do you call a room with no walls and no doors?

A A mushroom.

Keren S., aged 11

Q What's the tallest building in the world?

A A library – because it has so many stories!

Ho Suk Ji, aged 10

Andy's Funky Favourites

These are my favourites, obviously,
Monkeys and vomit, they fascinate me!
Matt on the floor and Art on the wall
Tell some of these – you'll have a ball ...

Q What's yellow and smells of Bananas?

A Monkey's vomit.   Oliver M., aged 4

Q What do you call a man nailed to a wall?

A Art.   Sally, aged 10

Q What do you call a man on the floor?

A Matt.   Luke T., aged 9

Q What do you call a man in a tree?

A Russell.   Peter V., aged 10

Q What do you call a man
floating in the ocean?

A Bob.   Simon E., aged 8

Q What do you call a deer with
no legs and no eyes?

A Still no eye dear.   Erica T., aged 10

Q What do you call a deer
with no eyes?

A No eye dear.
              Erica T., aged 10

Space Shots

Billions of stars like little dots,
Fired from the past like old space shots.
Pluto Pups and meteors spin through space,
Competing in a never ending race.

Q What game do spacemen play?
A Astronauts and crosses.   Sophie L., aged 11

Q What do you call a crazy spaceman?
A An astronut.   Peta R., aged 9

Q Where do astronauts go for fun?
A Lunar Park.   Kate J., aged 8

Q What do astronauts make
their underwear out of?
A Saturn.   Hannah L., aged 9

Q Where do astronauts leave their spaceships?

A At parking meteors. Ray P., aged 10

Q What's an astronaut's favourite chocolate?

A A Mars Bar. Kelly L., aged 9

Q What kind of dogs can astronauts eat?

A Pluto Pups. Shelby P., aged 9

Q What are bugs on the moon called?

A Lunatics. Lisa E., aged 9

Dinosaur and Dragon Ditties

Woolly mammoths on the floor,
Dragons smoking at the door.
Eggs sold at the dino-store,
Dragons sleeping, hear them snore.

Q What do you call a shop that sells dinosaurs?

A A dino-store.
Sarah T., aged 5

Q What did the egg say to the dinosaur?

A You're egg-stinct.
Courtney B., aged 7

Q What's the difference between dinosaurs and dragons?

A Dinosaurs are still too young to smoke.
Rodrigo I., aged 10

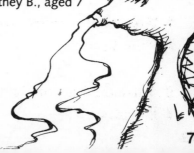

73

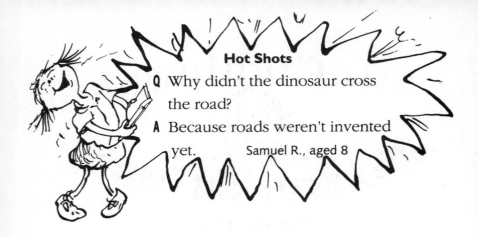

Hot Shots

Q Why didn't the dinosaur cross the road?

A Because roads weren't invented yet.

Samuel R., aged 8

Q Why are dragons big, red and scaly?

A Because if they were small, red and smooth, they'd be Smarties.

Caitlin P., aged 10

Q How do you know if there's a dragon under your bed?

A Your nose is touching the ceiling.

Frank L., aged 8

Q How do you know if there's a dragon in your soup?

A It's very lumpy.

Alexander L., aged 6

Comic

Conversations

**People are strange
In odd situations,
Especially when dribbling
Over comic conversations.**

Patient: 'What do the x-rays of my brain show?'
Doctor: 'Nothing.'   Erin T., aged 10

Three men walked into a bar.
Don't you think the third man
would have ducked?
      Andrew H., aged 9

Dad: 'Son, you have to go to school today.'
Son: 'I don't want to, everyone thinks I'm too bossy.'
Dad: 'But son, you have to go, you're the headmaster.'
      Matthew C., aged 8

'Doctor, Doctor, I snore so loudly I wake myself up.'
  'Then sleep in different rooms.'   Janelle F., aged 11

Hot Shots

'Waiter, what is this fly doing in my soup?'

'I believe it is doing freestyle.'

Evan S., aged 11

A man rushed into a doctor's surgery.

'Will you bandage my ear?' he asked.

He took a hanky from his head and showed the doctor that his ear was bleeding.

'What happened?' the doctor asked.

'I bit myself,' the man answered.

'That's impossible,' the doctor said, 'How in the world could you bite your own ear?'

'I was standing on a chair,' the man replied.

Kieran M., aged 9

Three men were having a competition to see who could drop their watch off a cliff, and run down and catch it before it hit the ground.

The first man dropped his watch, ran down and missed.

The second man dropped his watch over the cliff, ran down and fell, missing his watch also.

Then the third man threw his watch over the cliff, ran down and caught it. The other two asked him how he managed to catch his watch.

'Well, it was easy. My watch was two minutes slow.'

Kieran M., aged 9

Absolutely Stupid

Sometimes you laugh, sometimes you cry,
The joke is so stupid, you just don't know why.
But something about it tickles your chin,
Absolutely stupid guarantees a grin.

Q What bow doesn't tie?
A A rainbow.

Ashley B., aged 10

Q What is the easiest way to grow tall?
A Sleep long.

Melani V., aged 7

Q What's the cheapest way
to post somebody?
A A stamp on the foot.

Matthew C., aged 8

Q What do you call a man
without a shovel?
A Douglas.

Steven P., aged 6

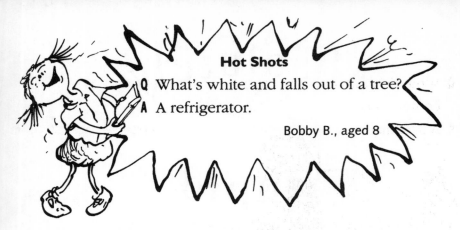

Hot Shots

Q What's white and falls out of a tree?
A A refrigerator.

Bobby B., aged 8

Q Who was the fastest runner at the Olympics?
A He was the one who lost his strides.

Tim G., aged 10

Q What would you do if the phone rang?
A Pick it up and put it down.

Amy G., aged 8

Q Why did the girl sleep with a ruler?
A She wanted to see how long she slept.

Janelle F., aged 11

Q What sort of nails can you find in shoes?
A Toenails.

Kali C., aged 9

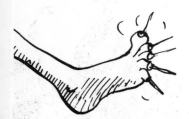

Q Where do chickens go when they die?
A To the oven.

Vanessa T., aged 7

Q What do you get if you cross a chicken with a cement mixer?

A A bricklayer.

Alistair M., aged 10

Q If teeth wore shoes, what sort would they be?

A Gumboots.

Peggy F., aged 7

Q 'Mum, will my pancake be long?'
A 'No, it will be round.'
Lara D., aged 8

Q What do you call a woman with a cat on her head?
A Kitty.
Hamish M., aged 7

Q What do you call a nut with a cold?
A Cashew.
Toni P., aged 9

'Doctor, Doctor, I think I need glasses.'
   'You certainly do, this is a butcher shop.'
Rosemary T., aged 8

Q What do you call a man with a car number plate on his head?
A Reg.
Warren R., aged 11

Sniffing

Snipes

**Your nose is a set of sniffing pipes,
and so are sneezed the sniffing snipes.**

Q What do you call a nose that plays music?
A A boogle.

Daniel L., aged 7

Q How did the dog smell with his nose cut off?
A Awful. Will D., aged 7

Q What is another name for a snail?
A A boogie with a crash helmet. Megan J., aged 11

Hot Shots

Q Why do people pick their noses?
A Because they can.

Cecilia M., aged 10

Q Where does the boogieman live?
A Up your nose.

Alex W., aged 9

Q What's green and red and sits in the corner?
A A bashed up boogie.

Steven P., aged 11

Farmyard

Funnies

**You never know where you'll meet a cow,
A chicken, a duck, or even a sow.
They all love to scratch their tummies,
And so were born the farmyard funnies.**

Q Where do sheep do their shopping?

A At Woollies.

Rebecca W., aged 10

Q What do cows drink?

A Cowpuccino.

Fatios M., aged 11

Hot Shots

Q What do you give a pig with cuts and bruises?
A Oinkment.   Phillipa D., aged 10

Q When is a vet in business?
A When it rains cats and dogs.   Krysten A., aged 8

Q What's a dog's favourite fruit?
A Pawpaw.   Mark G., aged 8

Q What do you call a big, muscular, good looking cow?
A A beefcake.   Jo-Anne F., aged 7

Q What do you call a cow with no legs?
A Ground beef.   Jeremy B., aged 10

Q What do you call a spooky dark horse?
A Nightmare.   Tegan L., aged 7

Q What is a dog's favourite TV show?
A A Dog's Tale.   Laura S., aged 10

84

How, Where, What & Why

Why is it so?
What could it be?
How do you know?
Well, just ask me ...

Q How can you see flying saucers?
A Trip a waiter.

Gisela J., aged 6

Q What do you call a man with a paper bag on his head?
A Russell.

Sam T., aged 9

Hot Shots

Q What do you call a man with a
Christmas tree on his head?

A Noel.   Susan R., aged 5

Q What do you call a man holding a rotten piece of meat?
A Graham.   Andrew P., aged 10

Q What do you call a man who owes money?
A Bill.   Samuel L., aged 8

Q What do call a man with really
short hair?
A Sean.

Rachel A., aged 7

Q What do you call a woman who comes out at night?
A Eve.   Tanya B., aged 6

Q How come hairdressers are never late for work?
A Because they take short cuts.   Kirri S., aged 10

Q How do you fix flat feet?
A Wear pumps.

Nicola H., aged 10

Q How do you get rid of
unwanted varnish?
A Take away the 'r' and it will
vanish.　　　Janelle F., aged 11

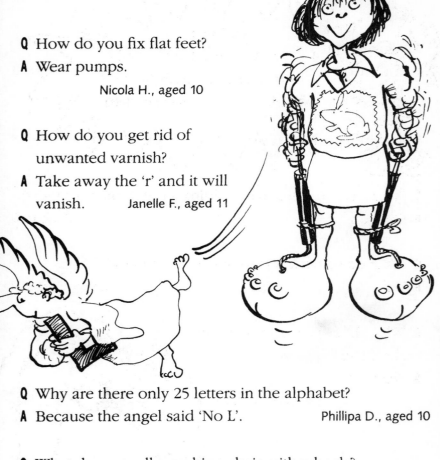

Q Why are there only 25 letters in the alphabet?
A Because the angel said 'No L'.　　　Phillipa D., aged 10

Q What do you call a rocking chair with wheels?
A A rock 'n' roller.　　　Jeremy P., aged 10

Q What did the big phone say to the little phone?

A You're too young to be engaged.   Nicholas P., aged 8

Q What goes in pink and comes out blue?

A A swimmer on a cold day.   Justin B., aged 7

Q What trees do hands grow on?

A Palm trees.   Ruben B., aged 7

Q Why did the boy want to walk on the moon?

A So he could moonwalk.   Anthony K., aged 8

Q What star can't shine at night?

A The sun.   Greg G., aged 7

Q Why did the hand cross the road?

A Because he wanted to go to the secondhand shop.

Alice H., aged 8

Witches, Fairies and Bears

Witches, fairies and bears, oh yeah!
Witches, fairies and bears, oh yeah!
Biddly, boddly, boo!

Q Why is *Play School* dangerous?
A Because there's a bear in there.

Kathryn R., aged 8

Q What does a bear wear when she's going to bed?
A The bear essentials.

Brian P., aged 9

Q What walks through the forest with sixteen legs?
A Snow White and the seven dwarfs.

Nathan L., aged 6

Q What do fairies use to clean their teeth?
A Fairy floss.

Deanne C., aged 6

Hot Shots

Q How do you make a witch itch?

A Take away her 'w'.

Hugh D., aged 8

Q How does a witch tell the time?

A With a witch watch.

Ania A., aged 10

Q Why did the bear knock
on the door upside down?

A Because he was on the roof.

Sam H., aged 10

Comic

Gastronomic

Bananas, oranges, apples and stew,
Peas and beans and apricots too.
You've gotta keep the rumbles away,
Your stomach needs food like a horse needs hay.

Q What did one fig say to the other fig?
A 'Wanna go on a date?'

Lucy L., aged 10

Q What's green and plays guitar?
A Elvis Parsley.

Kevin L., aged 9

Q Where do bakers keep their dough?
A In the bank.

Liam K., aged 7

Q What do you call an angry chocolate bar?
A A Violent Crumble.

Joshua L., aged 4

Q What made the icecream?
A Refrigerator II.

Gilbert H., aged 8

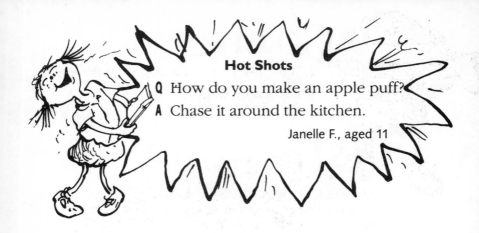

Hot Shots

Q How do you make an apple puff?

A Chase it around the kitchen.

Janelle F., aged 11

Q What food do robbers eat?

A Takeaway.   Leigh W., aged 7

Q Why did the potato cry?

A Because the chips were down.   Candice C., aged 9

Q What do you call a biscuit that's good at school?

A A smart cookie.   Bradley S., aged 7

Q What do you call a dog with no legs?
A A sausage dog.

Jenny N., aged 7

Q First there was the Ice Age, then there was the
Stone Age. What came next?
A The sausage.

Yonnie C., aged 10

Q What did the farmer call his two rows of cabbages?
A A dual cabbage way.

Morris W., aged 11

Q How do you start a pudding race?
A Sago.

Declan T., aged 9

Fishy Barbs

**Fishy tales
from the sea
will bring you laughing to your knees.**

Q What do you call a cat born in October?

A An octopus.

Rochelle I., aged 6

Q What type of fish live in blocks of units?

A Flatheads.

Kate J., aged 7

Q What makes you seasick?

A Your little brother's vomit.

Peter R., aged 10

Hot Shots

Q What sort of fish meow?

A Catfish.   Sarah T., aged 4

Q What do sea monsters eat?

A Fish and chips.

Anna A., aged 10

Q What do you call a goldfish on the floor?

A Carpet.   Jack P., aged 6

Q What do you call a wealthy fish?

A A goldfish.

Matthew C., aged 10

Q What do you call a fish that tunes pianos?

A Tuna.

Andy L., aged 6

PLINK
PLONK
SPLOSH

95

Jungle Jibes

From the darkest jungles of foreign lands,
Lions and tigers and singing Tarzans.
Exotic animals from many a tribe,
Ballawallawalla – jungle jibes!

Q What does Tarzan sing at Christmas?

A 'Jungle bells, jungle bells …'

Seran A., aged 7

Q What's green and swings through the trees?

A Tarzan the grape man.

Felix L., aged 9

Q Where do monkeys go on their holidays?

A To the Bananas.

Geraldine D., aged 5

Q What were Tarzan's last words?

A 'Who greased the vine?'

Alfred K., aged 8

Hot Shots

Q What sort of candy do monkeys eat?
A Monkey bars.   Anon.

Q What's black and white and eats like a horse?
A A zebra.   Julia W., aged 9

Q What do you call a lion on the floor?
A Lion-o.   Jack P., aged 6

Q What animal should you never play cards with?
A A cheetah.   Anthony J., aged 10

Q How do you know when an elephant has been in the fridge?
A There are footprints in the butter.   Scott R., aged 10

Q What do you get when you cross a monkey with a flower?
A A chimp-pansy.

                    Oscar R., aged 10

Hole in One

Tartan pants and bunker blues,
Dimpled balls hit with funny cues.
A hook or slice is second to none,
Unless of course, it's a hole in one.

Q Why do golf balls have dimples?
A Because they're cute.

Peter G., aged 9

Q Where do golf clubs live?
A In the club house.
Aimis L., aged

Q Why did the golfer wear two pairs of socks?
A In case he got a hole in one.
Luke T., aged

Q What sort of shirts do golfers wear?
A Tee-shirts.
Gehad T., aged

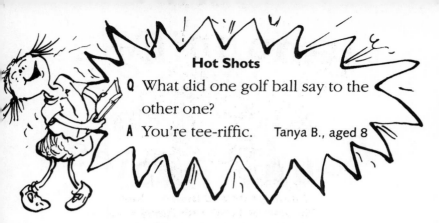

Hot Shots

Q What did one golf ball say to the other one?

A You're tee-riffic.   Tanya B., aged 8

Q What sort of cups do golfers drink out of?

A Tee-cups.   Josephine R., aged 7

Q What goes putt, putt, putt … putt … putt?

A A bad golfer.   Atticus H., aged 9

Bouncing

Bonny Babies

Boundless energy, those little bundles of joy,
Sometimes they scream and that can annoy.
But when they're asleep they're just so cute,
Bouncing bonny babies in their birthday suits.

Q What did Mr and Mrs Chicken call their baby?

A Egg.

Dussel H., aged 6

Q What did Mr and Mrs Ling call their baby duck?

A Duckling.

Tamara A., aged 11

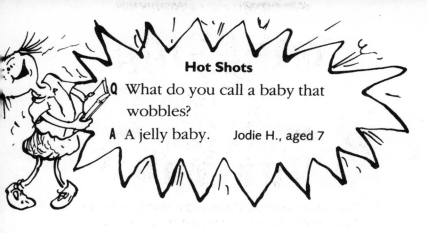

Hot Shots

Q What do you call a baby that wobbles?

A A jelly baby.   Jodie H., aged 7

Q What did Mr and Mrs Lette call their baby pig?

A Piglet.   Damon R., aged 8

Q What do you call a baby fly?

A Maggot.   Karen H., aged 7

Q What did the baby ant call his mother's sister?

A Anty.   Russel L., aged 8

Giggling

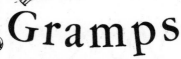

Gramps

He's old and wrinkled and kinda cute,
He wears a vest under his suit.
He sometimes complains of old age cramps,
The man we love – old giggling gramps.

Q What do you call a grandpa rowing a boat?
A Paddle-pop.

Adrian H., aged 8

Q What's your grandfather's favourite snack?
A Popcorn.

Jessica L., aged 6

Q What do you call your frozen grandfather?
A Popsicle.

Thomas P., aged 6

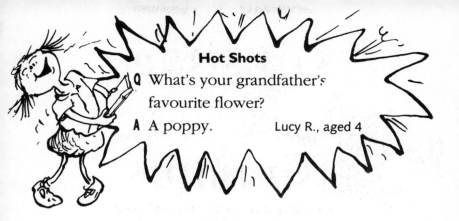

Q What's your grandfather's favourite flower?

A A poppy.

Lucy R., aged 4

Q What do you call your grandpa in space?

A Pop star.

Michael F., aged 10

Q What sound did the grandfather make when he exploded?

A Pop!

Michael M., aged 10

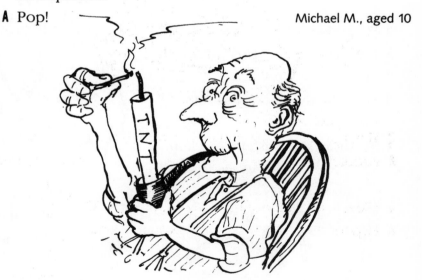

Q What did the big firecracker say to the little firecracker?

A My pop is bigger than your pop.

Marli S., aged 10

Feathered Funnies

Some can hoot and some can screech,
Some drop bombs at the beach.
Some animals you know sleep on their tummies,
And so you have the feathered funnies.

Q How do baby hens dance?
A Chick to chick.   Lucy B., aged 5

Q What do you call a dead parrot?
A Polygon.   Nigal H., aged 10

Q Why did the cockatoo cross
the road?
A To show she wasn't a chicken.

Valerie., aged 9

Q What do you call a good looking emu?
A Rare.   Ralf M., aged 11

Hot Shots

Q What bird can't you trust?

A A lyrebird.

Laura S., aged 10

Q What do you call a bird with a cold?

A A cocka-choo.

Felicity S., aged 7

CHOOO

Q What do you give a bird that is sick?

A Tweetment.

Paul L., aged 8

105

Q What did one owl say to the other owl at the disco?
A This is a hoot!

Dean S., aged !

Q What bird can cook?
A A kookaburra.

Benji C., aged 6

Q Which birds are religious?
A Birds of prey.

Angelica H., aged 1

Q Why did the chicken cross the road?
A For some fowl reason.

Andrew M., aged

Bugomania

Buggerly wuggerly sluggerly woo,
Slitherly slimerly slinkerly sloo.
Gets in your bed, crawls up your leg,
Drives you insane, help – Bugomania!

Q What do you get if you cross a centipede with a parrot?
A A walkie-talkie.   Brian H., aged 5

Q What lies around, one hundred feet up?
A A dead centipede.   Neil J., aged 9

Q Why do bees have sticky hair?
A Because they use honeycombs.   Zain K., aged 7

Hot Shots

Q What do you call an ant sitting on a $10 note?

A An antenna.   Madison S., aged 5

Q What did the famous fly say to the young starlet?

A Look out for me on the flyscreen.   Rebecca M., aged 9

Q Why do you feed cocoa to tadpoles?

A To make chocolate frogs.   Anna J., aged 7

Q What do you call a mosquito that likes cheese?

A Mozzie-rella.   Allira S., aged 6

Q What do you call four insects that play guitar?
A The Beetles. Robert F., aged 10

Q What do frogs sit on?
A Toadstools. Erin T., aged 10

Q Why couldn't the butterfly go to the dance?
A Because it was a moth ball. Angus R., aged 9

Q What did the mosquito say the first time it saw a camel's humps?
A 'Did I do that?' Jillian R., aged 7

Q What's red and has eight legs and four eyes?
A I don't know, but it's on your shoulder.

Michael V., aged 6

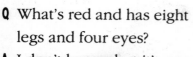

Q Why are mosquitoes religious?

A Because they sing over you before they prey on you.

Erica D., aged 8

Q How do you start a flea race?

A One, two, flea, go!

Patricia D., aged 10

PHEEEEEEEP

Q Where do frogs keep their money?

A In the riverbank.

Oliver H., aged 10

Q What goes through a grasshopper's mind when he hits the windscreen of a car at 100 km per hour?

A His legs.

Kent C., aged 11

Egg-Straordinary

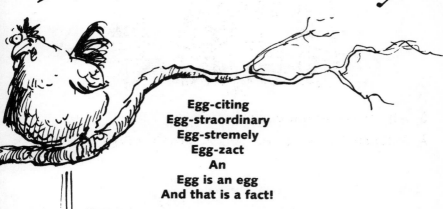

**Egg-citing
Egg-straordinary
Egg-stremely
Egg-zact
An
Egg is an egg
And that is a fact!**

Q How do you know when an egg is getting on in the world?

A When it's on a roll.

Anthony J., aged 11

Q What did one egg say to the other?

A You're cracked.

Victor P., aged 5

Q What do you call an egg that knows everything?

A An egg-spert.

Ciara M., aged 7

egg-spert

Q What do you call a hatched egg?

A A cute chick.

Paul L., aged 8

Hot Shots

Q What do you call a silly egg?
A Egg-nog.

Penny P., aged 7

Q What do you call an egg in the air?
A Unlucky.

Jennifer C., aged 5

Q Why did the egg cross the road?
A Because Humpty Dumpty was indisposed.

Lisa F., aged 10

Q What do you call two eggs in the frying pan?
A Fried eggs.

Robert F., aged 6

Q What's the biggest takeaway egg-store in the world?
A MacEggnolds.

John F.J., aged 7

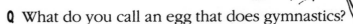

Q What do you call an egg that does gymnastics?
A An eggflip.

Chris J., aged 5

Q What did the old egg say to the young egg?
A Life is a wonderful egg-sperience.

Olivia S., aged 10

Q What do you call twelve eggs in the mud?
A The Dirty Dozen.

Bradley J., aged 5

Doctor, Doctor!

**Doctor, Doctor, tell me why
I've two noses, and one eye.
Is it something I have eaten?
Tell me please, is there treatment?**

'Doctor, Doctor, I've lost my memory.'
  'When did this happen?'
  'I can't remember.'

Keith L., aged 12

'Doctor, Doctor, I feel like a cricket ball.'
  'How's that?'
  'Oh no! Not you as well!'

Robert S., aged 11

'Doctor, Doctor, I've got bananas growing out of my ears.'
  'Oh, no, how did this happen?'
  'I don't know, I planted apples.'

Warren R., aged 12

'Doctor, Doctor, my aunt has a sore throat.'
'Give her this bottle of auntie-septic.' Rachel T., aged 7

'Doctor, Doctor, can you give me something for wind?'
'Yes – here's a kite.' Aaron W., aged 8

Colour Coordinated

**What's yellow and red and black and green?
It's colour coordinated,
It's a scream!**

Q If a buttercup is yellow, what colour is a hiccup?
A Burple.
Lennie T., aged 8

Q What's green and prickly and goes up and down?
A A kiwi fruit in a lift.
Tonya R., aged 9

Q When is a green book not a green book?
A When it's read.
Tiffany V., aged 6

Q What's green and mouldy and runs through the forest?
A Mouldy Locks.
Anthony K., aged 7

115

Hot Shots

Q What's black and white and very noisy?

A A magpie with a set of drums.

Joshua L., aged 8

Q What's green with red spots?

A A frog with measles.

Pippa G., aged 7

Q What's grey and white and red all over?

A An embarrassed elephant.

Kylie P., aged 9

Aussie-a-Rama

**We have Ayers Rock and Sydney Harbour
Lightning Ridge and Kakadu.
We have emus and koalas,
And the great red kangaroo.**

Q What did the didgeridoo?
A Went to see the boomerang. Indianna R., aged 7

Q Why did the city boy go to the outback?
A He wanted to see a barn dance. Rodney L., aged 10

Q What pies can fly?
A Magpies. Steven A., aged 7

Hot Shots

Q How do you get rid of a boomerang?
A Throw it down a one way street.

Kristy H., aged 10

Q What do you get when you cross a koala with a kangaroo?
A A fur coat with big pockets.

Danny K., aged 10

Q What do kangaroos have that no other animals have?
A Baby kangaroos.

Tyson A., aged 10

Q How come koalas carry their babies on their backs?
A They can't push a pram up a tree.

Courtney H., aged 6

Q Where do you take a kangaroo with bad eyesight?
A The hoptician.

Megan R., aged 11

118

Occupational

Hazards

Day after
Day after
Day after
Day after
Day after
Day after
Day – there's got to be
more to life than this ...
let's have some fun!

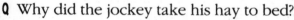

Q Why did the jockey take his hay to bed?
A He wanted to feed his nightmares.

Paul K., aged 6

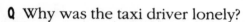

Q Why was the taxi driver lonely?
A Because he drove all his customers away.

Madelin B., aged 6

Q What do you call a flying policeman?
A A heli-copper.

Maxwell L., aged 7

Hot Shots

Q What person do you always take your hat off to?

A A barber.

Sophie R., aged 10

Q Why did the baker stop making doughnuts?

A Because he got tired of the hole business.   Laura L., aged 9

Q Who gets the sack every time they go to work?

A The postie.

Thomas V., aged 9

Q What was the lawyer's name?

A Sue.

Stephanie H., aged 7

Q What happened to the composer who took too many long baths?

A He started writing operas.   Monica W., aged 12

Q What sport do judges play?

A Tennis – because it's played in a court.

Hayley R., aged 10

120

In Your Mouth

You have lips that pout,
And teeth that chew.
A tongue that licks,
And taste buds too.

Q What do you do when your tooth falls out?
A Use toothpaste.

Vennesa W., aged 6

Q What's a tooth fairy's favourite food?
A Gumnuts.

Theo P., aged 7

Q What trees do teeth grow on?
A Gum trees.

Amy L., aged 6

Q How do tooth fairies get around?

A On chew chew trains.

Niamh B., aged 8

Q What do get if you cross a dentist with an elephant?

A Gumbo.

Sophie G., aged 7

Q What is the best thing to put into a pie?

A Your teeth.

Candice C., aged 8

Spook-o-Moondo

Ghosts and monsters, skeletons and ghouls,
They'll trick you – they're nobody's fools.
Scaring you is what they like,
Screaming and moaning, they'll give you a fright.

Q What do call a skeleton who tells jokes?
A Funny Bones.

Debbie S., aged 6

Q What do ghosts like to eat for dinner?
A Spook-ghetti.

Leon A., aged 9

Q What type of glasses does a ghost wear?
A Spook-tacles.

Leon A., aged 9

123

Q How do skeletons call each other?
A On the tele-bone. Vincent T., aged 6

Q What do you call a single vampire?
A A bat-chelor. Javier P., aged 9

Q What's a skeleton's favourite instrument?
A Saxa-bone. Lucy R., aged 6

Q Why does a monster need three lenses in his glasses?
A Because he has three eyes. Stuart C., aged 10

Q What kind of mistakes do ghosts make?
A Boo-boos. Pepe R., aged 7

Q What's a ghost's favourite bird?
A A scarecrow. Nicholas F., aged 9

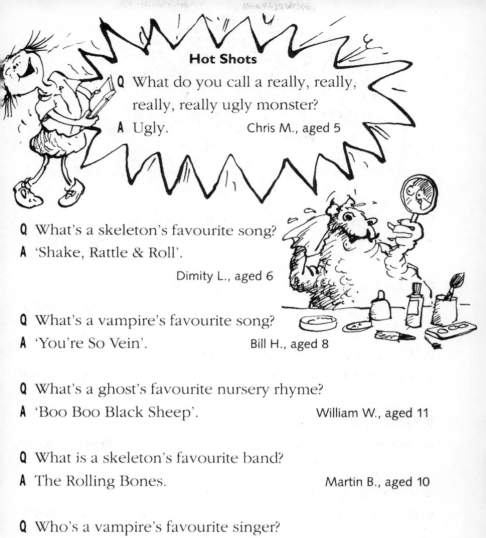

Hot Shots

Q What do you call a really, really, really, really ugly monster?

A Ugly.   Chris M., aged 5

Q What's a skeleton's favourite song?

A 'Shake, Rattle & Roll'.

Dimity L., aged 6

Q What's a vampire's favourite song?

A 'You're So Vein'.   Bill H., aged 8

Q What's a ghost's favourite nursery rhyme?

A 'Boo Boo Black Sheep'.   William W., aged 11

Q What is a skeleton's favourite band?

A The Rolling Bones.   Martin B., aged 10

Q Who's a vampire's favourite singer?

A K.D. Fang.   Martina R., aged 12

Q What's a vampire's favourite dog?

A A bloodhound.   Jasmine C., aged 11

Q How does a ghost tell his future?
A By reading his horrorscope.
Ezra K., aged 9

Q What does a vampire put at the end of a sentence?
A A full clot.
Wendy H., aged 9

Q What's a ghost's favourite musical?
A Phantom of the Opera.
Clare C., aged 11

Q What do ghosts put on their roast beef?
A Gravey.
Veronica P., aged 9

Q What's a ghost's favourite party game?
A Haunt and Seek.
Shelby N., aged 10

Q What do ghosts like to do at parties?
A Boogie.
Jiddic P., aged 12

Knock, Knock ...

**Knock, knock, knock,
My name is Giraffe.
These jokes are here
to make you laugh!**

Knock, knock!
Who's there?
Hannah.
Hannah who?
Hannah's a sandwich, I'm a bit hungry.   Paul G., aged 9

Knock, knock!
Who's there?
Gotter.
Gotter who?
Gotter go to the toilet.
    Amanda B., aged 7

Knock, knock!
Who's there?
Daisy.
Daisy who?
Daisy plays, nightsy sleeps.   Michelle L., aged 7

Knock, knock!
Who's there?
Eddie.
Eddie who?
Eddie body there?

Will D., aged 7

Knock, knock!
Who's there?
Ivor.
Ivor who?
Ivor cold today.

Alice P., aged 7

Knock, knock!
Who's there?
Keith.
Keith who?
Keith me thweetheart.

Sky B., aged 4

Knock, knock!
Who's there?
Emma.
Emma who?
Emma bit late, sorry.

Lavern T., aged 8

Knock, knock!
Who's there?
Olive.
Olive who?
Olive across the road.

James D., aged 8

Knock, knock!
Who's there?
Donna.
Donna who?
Donna open the door or I'll get you!   Andrea S., aged 9

Knock, knock!
Who's there?
Luke.
Luke who?
Luke through the key hole and you'll see.   Benjamin J., aged 7

Knock, knock!
Who's there?
William.
William who?
Williamind your own business.   Carly S., aged 9

Knock, knock!
Who's there?
Ken.
Ken who?
Ken I come in?
    Jared P., aged 6

Andy's Monkey's Funky Favourites

Q What's green and smells of eucalyptus?
A Koala vomit. Andrew D., aged 6

Q What do you call a man with an elephant on his head?
A Squashed. Dennis P., aged 8

Q 'Mum, can I have a budgie for Christmas?'
A 'No, you'll have turkey like the rest of us!' Sean S., aged 10

Q What's a crocodile's favourite card game?
A Snap. Annabell P., aged 6

Q What flies and wobbles?
A A jellycopter. Aralia P., aged 8

Peas Please

Little green things
That roll with ease
Can you pass me
The Peas Please

Q. What do you call an angry pea?
A. Grum-pea

Melissa T. aged 10

Q. What do you call a smiling pea?
A. Hap-pea

Samuel E. aged 9

Q. What do you call a pea that bites?
A. Nip-pea

Teresa L. aged 10

Q. What do you call a pea with goose bumps?
A. Lump-pea

Joshua C. aged 9

Q. What do you call a clean pea?
A. Soap-pea

Kelly S. aged 8

Q. What do you call a nervous pea?

A. Jump-pea

Billy R. aged 10

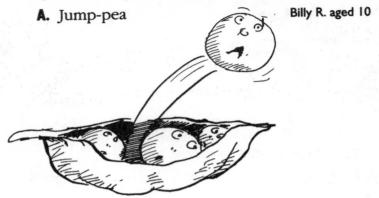

Q. What do peas wear on their lips?

A. Lip-pea

Violetta S. aged 6

Q. What do you call a crazy pea?

A. Loop-pea

Oliver L. aged 10

Q. What do baby peas wear?

A. Nap-peas

Isabella T. aged 9

Q. What's a pea's favourite sport?
A. Fris-pea
Elaine R. aged 10

Q. What do you call an exhausted pea?
A. Sleep-pea
Rachel V. aged 9

Q. What do you call a pea with mud on it?
A. Swamp-pea
Hamish H. aged 7

Q. What do you call an old pea?
A. Droop-pea
Joshua M. aged 7

Q. What do you call a silly pea?
A. Dope-pea
Max L. aged 9

Q. What's a pea's favourite drink?
A. A slur-pea
Keith M. aged 7

D-D-D-Dance

Tango or twist
In a rhythmic trance
Slave to the beat
D-D-D-Dance

Q. What type of dancing do you do in an amusement parlour?

A. Pin-ball dancing   Ivanah L. aged 9

Q. What's a mummy's favourite dance?

A. Wrap   David K. aged 9

Q. What dance do you get if you cross a fox and a horse?

A. The fox-trot   Matthew L. aged 7

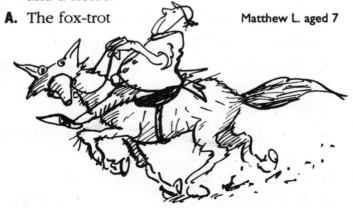

Q. What's a lion's favourite dance?
A. Lion-dancing

Jayden M. aged 8

Q. What type of dancing has a lounge, a
kitchen, a bathroom, and a bedroom?
A. House-dancing

Monique E. aged 10

Q. Where do you study dancing?
A. At the disco-tech

Sarah M. aged 10

Q. What do you call a funky quacker?
A. A disco duck

Grant P. aged 9

Q. What is a monkey's favourite dance?
A. The orang-a-tango   Mark J. aged 7

Q. What sort of jockey do you see at the disco?
A. A disc-jockey   Melissa M. aged 8

Q. What does a ballet dancing hippo wear?
A. A 20-20   Natalie B. aged 10

Sporty Sprongs

Footy and golf
Jumps so long
Quick as a flash
Sporty Sprongs

Q. Why did the jogger go to the vet?
A. Because his calves hurt

Jess P. aged 7

Q. When does a high jumper jump highest?
A. In a leap year

Kane R. aged 9

Q. What do you get when you cross a computer programmer with an athlete?
A. A floppy diskus thrower

Peeda L. aged 8

Q. What happens when cricketers get old?
A. They go batty

Clint A. aged 11

Q. What's a baby's favourite swimming stroke?

A. Australian crawl

Panta Z. aged 6

Q. Why did all the bowling pins go down?

A. Because they were on strike

Senita P. aged 6

Q. How do people with the flu get exercise?

A. When their noses run Jacinta R. aged 12

Q. What's the difference between a musician and a cricketer?

A. One scores a hit, the other hits a score

Greg L. aged 6

Q. Why did the man jog around his bed?

A. He wanted to catch up on his sleep

Lucy T. aged 5

Christmas Capers

Santa's team of
Elf toy makers
Always deliver
Christmas Capers

Q. What's Santa Claus's wife called?

A. Mary Christmas   Joe C. aged 10

Q. Where does Santa go on holidays?

A. Ho Ho Hobart   Christopher J. aged 6

Q. What did Adam say on the day before Christmas?

A. 'It's Christmas, Eve'   Filomena M. aged 10

Q. What do you get if you cross Santa with a tiger?
A. Santa Claws

Jamille T. aged 6

Q. What's red, white and black, and taps on the window?
A. Santa Claus in the microwave

Michelle M. aged 11

Q. What is rude and only comes at Christmas?
A. Rude-olf

Pam K. aged 9

Q. What's Santa's favourite vegetable?
A. Holly-flower

Anthony C. aged 10

HOLLY-FLOWER CHEESE

Bunny Funnies

**Cutesy ears and
Funny tummies
I just love the
Bunny Funnies**

Q. What is rabbit's favourite dance?

A. The bunny hop — Adam R. aged 6

Q. What do you call a rabbit with fleas?

A. Bugs bunny — Mitchell C. aged 5

Q. Why can't a bunny's nose be 12 inches long?

A. Because then it would be a foot — Agatha H. aged 12

Q. What do you call a rabbit that tells jokes?

A. A funny-bunny — Angharad M. aged 7

Q. What kind of jewellery do rabbits like to wear?
A. 24 carrot gold   Jarad S. aged 6

Q. What does a boy rabbit call a girl rabbit?
A. A honey-bunny   Christian S. aged 10

Q. How do you say 'Richard and Robert have
   a rabbit', without using the 'R' sound?
A. Dick and Bob have a bunny   Dave B. aged 9

Q. How is the rabbit who swallowed 50c?
A. No change yet   Holly C. aged 9

Q. How do rabbits travel?
A. By hare-plane   Oliver P. aged 7

Lolly Gags

**Reach within
the sweetest bags
then withdraw
The Lolly Gags**

Q. What's a dog's favourite lolly?
A. A Lick-o-rish   Peta P. aged 10

Q. What sort of babies do monsters eat?
A. Jelly-babies   Maria F. aged 9

Q. What's an octopus's favourite lolly?
A. A jelly bean   Trong H. aged 10

Q. What do you call a lolly from Europe?
A. A Malteser   Tony H. aged 9

Q. What do you call a lolly that tells jokes?
A. A lolly-gag   Kate J. aged 10

Q. What's a pigeon's favourite lolly?
A. A fan-tail   Nick J. aged 11

Q. What sort of lollys do koalas eat?
A. Chewing gum   Annabella H. aged 10

Q. What do you call a sensitive lolly?
A. Marshmallow   Shirley P. aged 12

Q. What's your grandfather's favourite sweet?
A. A lolly-pop   Rebecca C. aged 5

Q. What lolly is always late?
A. Choc-o-late   Swee N. aged 10

Q. What's a heavy metal band's favourite lolly?

A. Rocky Road

Leoni V. aged 6

Q. What weighs two tonnes, feels cold and comes on a stick?

A. A hippopopsicle Sung H. aged 7

Q. What sort of chocolate do cowboys eat?

A. Wagon-wheels

Francis T. aged 10

Nifty Names

Goldie and Gidget
Flash and James
You just can't beat
Nifty Names

Q. What sort of food do Tims eat?

A. Tim-Tams

Kelly-Ann B. aged 10

Q. What type of jumpers do Joes wear?

A. Sloppy-Joes

Rob L. aged 6

Q. Where do Jims exercise?

A. The Jim-nasium

Taren C. aged 7

Q. What do you call a crazy girl?

A. Maddy

Petra Z. aged 10

Q. What do you get if you cross a donkey, a Donna and a baby?

A. A Donna-ke-bub

Theo P. aged 11

Q. What do you call a June in the desert?

A. A sand-June

Liam L. aged 10

Q. What do you get if you cross the inside of an apple and a car?

A. A Cortina

Sam N. aged 10

Cryptic Teasers

Out of the vault
Into the freezer
Brain sucking puzzles
Cryptic Teasers

Q. What happens when you kiss a clock?

A. Your lips-tick

James K. aged 7

One One was a racehorse
Two Two was one too
One One won one race
Two Two won one too

Karen H. and Kristy L. aged 11

Q. Where do you find the most fish?

A. Between the head and the tail   Nicola aged 5

Q. What gets lost every time you stand up?

A. Your lap   Emily G. aged 7

Q. What has four legs and doesn't walk?

A. A table   Joshua John A. aged 7

Q. What comes once in a minute, twice in a moment and not in a thousand years?

A. The letter 'M'   Amanda H. aged 8

Q. What's the brain-sucker doing on your head?

A. Wasting its time

Jason P. aged 10

Q. What is the worst day for a fish?

A. Fryday

Evan F. aged 11

MUM: Sally, why aren't you going to school today?

SALLY: Because yesterday my teacher said that $4 + 1 = 5$ and $2 + 3 = 5$ and $5 + 0 = 5$

MUM: So?

SALLY: Well, I'm not going back until he makes up his mind

Kandas M. aged 10

Q. What do you do if you are stuck in the desert?

A. Take off your watch and drink from the
spring and eat the sand-wich is all around you

Mark T. aged 10

Q. What planet has the biggest bottom?

A. Sat-on   Matthew C. aged 10

Q. Why did the clock go to hospital?

A. Because he had a tick on him   Josie H. aged 9

Q. What would you do if a truck ran over your toe?

A. Call a toe-truck   Tim P. aged 8

Twisted Travel

**Ships and planes and trains
Unravel,
Lets go and do some
Twisted Travel**

Q. What kind of fish do they serve on aeroplanes?

A. Flying fish

Kevin C. aged 6

Q. What's the best way to cross a moat?

A. In a moater-boat

Tina L. aged 6

Q. What member of the ship's crew packs away the playing cards?

A. The deckhand
Dennis B. aged 11

Q. Why do fishers use helicopters?

A. 'Cause the whirly bird gets the worm

Maggie B. aged 11

Q. What is a ship builder's favourite meal?

A. Launch
Mia U. aged 11

Q. What kind of elephant flys a jet?

A. A Jumbo
Max L. aged 10

Band-e-monium

A caucophony of sounds
An echoing podium
Music and mirth
It's pandemonium

Q. What kind of phones do musicians use?
A. A saxophone

Amelia A. aged 10

Q. What's a dog's favourite music?
A. Trom-bone music

Mark G. aged 9

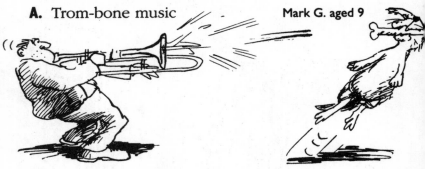

Q. What kind of crabs play music?
A. Fiddler crabs

Craig S. aged 9

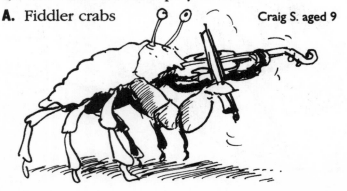

Q. Who's a monster's favourite singer?

A. Mariah Hairy

Carolyn T. aged 10

Q. What instrument does a nagging sister play?

A. The harp

Alexandra X. aged 11

Q. What's the maths teacher's favourite instrument?

A. The triangle

Phillip R. aged 8

Q. What does your nanna play records on?

A. The Gran-ma phone

Melissa B. aged 7

Q. Where do you find a musical cat?

A. Sing-a-paw

Roberta S. aged 6

Scintillating Science

**From natural phenomena
To the kitchen appliance
So is the birth
Of Scintillating Science**

Q. What did one atom say to the other?
A. Nothing, atoms can't talk   Patricia F. aged 10

Q. If an electric train goes 250 kilometres per
hour, which way does the smoke go?
A. Electric trains don't blow smoke   Robbie D. aged 11

Q. What trees like a warm beverage?

A. Tea-trees

Ashley H. aged 9

Q. What's a volcano?

A. A mountain with hiccups

Owen P. aged 10

Q. Why do birds fly south for the winter?

A. 'Cause it's too far to walk

Jenna H. aged 10

Q. What did one magnet say to the other?

A. I find you very attractive

Patricia F. aged 10

Q. What did the scientists prove when they found bones on the moon?

A. The cow didn't make it

Kylie N. aged 12

Q. Which is lighter, the sun or the Earth?

A. The sun, 'cause it rises every morning

Steven L. aged 7

Rag Gags

Dress for success
Don't be a dag
Always be prepared
With a Rag Gag

Q. What type of pants do scientists wear?
A. Genes

Kathleen P. aged 6

Q. What sort of hat does a spy wear?
A. A peek-cap

Helen D. aged 6

Q. What type of underwear do zebras wear?
A. Z-bras

Danielle A. aged 7

Q. What did the boulder wear to the party?
A. A F-rock

Penelope O. aged 7

Q. What do pigs wear to bed?
A. Pig-jamas

Karen H. aged 11

Q. What type of suit does a duck wear?

A. A duxedo   Pai Jayne L. aged 10

Q. What does a house wear?

A. A-dress   Zena P. aged 10

Q. What do you call pants from Australia?

A. Down underpants   Jason F. aged 6

Burps and Slurps
and Snorts and Sneezes

Burps are Babulous
Slurps are Sluperb
Snorts are Snerific
Sneezes are Absurd

Q. What was the loudest dinosaur?

A. A Burposaurus Rex

Kieren O. aged 5

Burp

Q. What did Mozart get when he ate baked beans?

A. Classical gas   Danny M. aged 8

Q. What do you call an attractive pig?
A. A good snort

Kelly J. aged 8

Q. What kind of snacks do noses like?
A. Sneezels

Sarah W. aged 6

Q. What do you call a monster that lives in your mouth?
A. A Troll-ey-Golly

Ryan B. aged 10

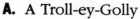

Monster Madness

It's with regret
Angst and sadness
I submit to
Monster Madness

Q. How does the abominable snowman get around?
A. By-icicle   Jane N. aged 5

Q. How does a three-legged monster get around?
A. By Tri-cycle   Candice K. aged 6

Q. How do monsters like their eggs?
A. Terri-fried   Carmel B. aged 6

Q. What's a monster's favourite part of the newspaper?

A. Horror-scope   Bill F. aged 7

Q. What do you call a city monsters live in?

A. A Monstros-city   David C. aged 6

Q. What do you call the winner of a monster beauty contest?

A. Ugly

Dan B. aged 8

Q. What do you call a monster who eats his father's sister?

A. An Aunt-eater

Emily A. aged 12

Q. How does a monster count to 13?

A. On his fingers

Brad R. aged 10

Q. Who's a monster's favourite singer?

A. Kylie Min-ogre

Kenneth A. aged 10

Q. Why did the monster bury his battery?

A. Because it was dead

Seraphina L. aged 10

Q. What would you get if you crossed a monster with a dozen eggs?

A. A very hairy omelette

Owen P. aged 10

Brains of Jello

The sky is blue
The sun is yellow
These jokes were made
By Brains of Jello

Q. Why did the man give up tap dancing?

A. 'Cause he kept falling down the sink

Lizzie S. aged 8

Q. Why did the banana split?

A. Because he saw the bread box, the milkshake and the egg beat   Tegan H. aged 10

Q. What did one frog say to another when they jumped into the river?

A. Knee-deep, Knee-deep, Knee-deep!

Kaitlin E. aged 7

Q. What does a frog say when he washes the car?

A. Rub it, Rub it, Rub it.

Evan F. aged 11

Q. What did the frog say when he walked into the library?

A. Read it, Read it, Read it.

Bryn S. aged 8

Bovine Hilarity

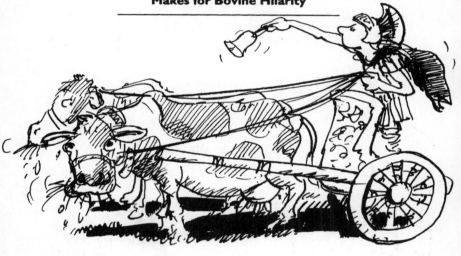

**Cows eat grass
It's no charity
Eating meat
Makes for Bovine Hilarity**

Q. Why do cows have bells?
A. Because their horns don't work   Rada L. aged 9

Q. What do cows eat for breakfast?
A. Mooslie   Lizzie S. aged 8

Q. What do the mummy cows do to the baby
cows at night?
A. Give them a cowslick and pat them off to
moo-moo land   Rodney S. aged 8

Q. Who is a cow's favourite singer?

A. Moo Donna Tahna S. aged 11

Q. Which cow is the smartest?

A. A mathemootician Tahna S. aged 11

Q. Where do cowstronauts go?

A. The mooooon Andrew L. aged 10

Q. What did the shopkeeper say to the cow?

A. Do you want this one or the udder? Alastaire R. aged 9

Q. Where do cows go out?

A. Discow dancing! Nigel L. aged 10

Q. What do you call a cow that watches lots of TV?

A. A cow-ch potato Elenor H. aged 10

Q. What's a cow's favourite hairdo?

A. A cowslick Ishbel N. aged 9

Q. What is a cow's favourite article of clothing?
A. Udder pants   Patrick S. aged 8

Q. What do you call a cow riding a skateboard?
A. A cow-tastrophy about to happen

                                            Max E. aged 7

Q. Where do cows go on holidays?
A. Moo-moo land   Joanne P. aged 10

Vroom Vroom

**Vroom Vroom
A puff of smoke
Fasten your seatbelt
It's Auto Jokes**

Q. What kind of cars do toads drive?
A. Hop rods

Peter G. aged 6

SPEED
90 - 0
0 - 90
90 - 0
0 - 90

Q. What's the best numberplate in the world?

A. 'X L R 8'   Henry B. aged 10

Q. What do you give a sick car?
A. A fuel injection   Lisa F. aged 9

Q. What do you call an expensive car with a cheap name?
A. A poor-sche   Phillip P. aged 9

Q. What do get if you cross a car with a dress?
A. A Mini skirt   Fatima F. aged 10

Q. What's the funniest car in the world?
A. A Jokes wagon   Bennita H. aged 7

Q. What type of car did Elvis Presley drive?
A. A Rock-n-Roll Royce   Sharne D. aged 11

Q. What would happen if everyone had a pink car?
A. We'd have a pink car-nation   Kylie N. aged 12

Tubular Tales

Over the sand
Wind in your sails
Let us prepare
For Tubular Tales

Q. How many surfers does it take to change a light bulb?

A. 'Hey man! What light bulb?' Eric L. aged 10

Q. What's a surfer's favourite hairstyle?

A. A vertical cut back Emma H. aged 7

Q. Why do surfers wear wet suits?

A. 'Cause dry-suits aren't invented yet

Nicholas L. aged 7

Q. What do surfers and candles have in common?
A. They both have wax heads   Deeb F. aged 6

Q. Why are surfers like plumbers?
A. They both dig the pipeline   John O. aged 10

Q. Why do surfers wear board shorts?
A. 'Cause busy shorts don't have the time

Madeline A. aged 9

Q. Why did the surfer cry?
A. Because the sea-weed   Guiseppe S. aged 6

Q. What's the best way to surf the net?
A. Buy a computer   Nathan B. aged 6

Q. How do you land surf?
A. Do a Mexican wave   Tyson K. aged 8

Q. What is a surfer's favourite song?
A. Roll out the barrel   Marnie V. aged 12

Little Brother

A beastie appeared
Like no other
A mini menace
My Little Brother

Q. Why do little brothers chew with their mouths open?

A. Flies have gotta live somewhere Piers F. aged 9

Q. What's small, annoying and really ugly?

A. I don't know, but it comes when I call out my little brother's name Vini S. aged 10

Q. How do you hurt your little brother's finger?

A. Smack him in the nose

Samantha T. aged 7

Q. What do flies and little brothers have in common?

A. They both vomit a lot and keep coming back

Freda Q. aged 9

Q. How do you make your little brother run?

A. Say 'bath time!' Victor R. aged 9

Q. How do you get your little
    brother to come when called?
A. 'Hey, Rodent'   Steven M. aged 12

Q. What's worse than one little brother?
A. Two little brothers   Michael L. aged 10

Q. How do you know when your little brother
    is in the room?
A. Listen for scratching sounds   Vanessa W. aged 6

Q. How do you confuse your little brother?
A. Call out his name   Martha M. aged 8

Q. What squeaks and burps
    when you sit on it?
A. Your little brother

          Brian F. aged 10

Knock Knock

Knock Knock
Who is there?
I opened the door
In my underwear

Knock, Knock
Who's there?
Fang
Fang who?
Fang you very much
Trudi Anne M. aged 10

Knock, Knock
Who's there?
Funny
Funny who?
Funny the way you keep saying 'who's there?'
every time I knock   Kiahnee Fay L. aged 10

Knock, Knock
Who's there?
Alaska
Alaska who?
Alaska no questions
I tella no lies   Kara B. aged 7

179

Knock, Knock
Who's there?
Jane
Jane who?
Time to Jane your clothes

Melissa F. aged 10

Knock, Knock
Who's there?
Eggbert
Eggbert who?
Egg but no bacon   Tom H. aged 9

Knock, Knock
Who's there?
Will
Will who?
Will you sit down and shut up   Matthew F. aged 10

Knock, Knock
Who's there?
Egg
Egg who?
Eggslent
Stephanie B. aged 8

Knock, Knock
Who's there?
Betty
Betty who?
Betty late than never   David K. aged 7

Knock, Knock
Who's there?
Lie since
Lie since who?
I haven't told you a lie since I was 10

Louise P. aged 12

Knock, Knock
Who's there?
Nick
Nick who?
Nick off   Emily P. aged 6

Knock, Knock
Who's there?
Ya
Ya who?
Didn't know there was a cowboy in the room!
Patrick C. aged 3

Knock, Knock
Who's there?
Kermit
Kermit who?
Kermit a robbery and you end up in jail

Paul R. aged 7

Fruity Follies

Up with health
Down with lollies
Let's start chewing
Fruity Follies

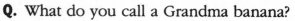

Q. What do you call a Grandma banana?
A. Nana

Zureka G. aged 10

Q. Who is the god of all bananas?
A. Banana-Rama

Laura P. aged 12

Q. How do gorillas play pool?
A. With a cue-cumber

Leslie N. aged 7

Q. What do you call a vegetable kiss?
A. Gar-lick

Matt V. aged 9

Q. What's the heaviest vegetable in the world?

A. Squash
Margaret N. aged 8

Q. What does one orange call another?

A. Orange
Bradley S. aged 7

Q. How do you know when an apple is sick?

A. It's rotten to the core
Geoff P. aged 8

Q. What fruit swings in the trees?
A. Tarzan the Grape-man

David L. aged 6

Q. What fruit always comes back?
A. A Bananarang   Sonia W. aged 9

Q. What do you call a retired vegetable?
A. A has-bean   Andrew P. aged 10

Q. Why did the tomato stop in the middle of the road?
A. He wanted to play squash   Merconi V. aged 8

Q. What do you call a really, really strong vegetable?
A. Vegemite   Suzannah W. aged 9

Q. When corncobs play cricket, what does the bowler bowl?
A. Corn balls   Jesse S. aged 7

Q. Which city was the capital of the corn civilisation?
A. Cornstantinople   Jesse S. aged 7

Q. What do you call an overweight plum?
A. Plump   Marcus P. aged 5

Q. What happens when you step on grapes?

A. They wine   Peter H. aged 6

Q. What is yellow, looks like a banana, smells like a banana and lies at the bottom of a tree?

A. Monkey's vomit   Kylie M. aged 9

Q. What do you get when you cross a pine tree with an apple tree?

A. A pineapple tree   Wesley F. aged 9

Q. What do you get if you cross a lemon with a cat?

A. A sour-puss   Tina D. aged 10

Souled Out

Multiple-eyed
Two tongues to tout
Walk on brother
It's Souled Out!

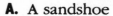

Q. What runs along with you, then lies under your bed with its tongue hanging out?

A. A sandshoe

Alexander F. aged 6

Q. What has twenty eyes, four tongues and smells?

A. Your running shoes

Sarah R. aged 11

Q. What kind of shoes do frogs wear?

A. Open toad shoes

Anson T. aged 6

Q. What do you call a shoe that swims in the sea?

A. Slipper

Freya H. aged 9

Q. What kind of shoes do caveman wear?

A. Ugh boots

Caitlyn G. aged 10

Q. What kind of shoes do camels wear?

A. Desert boots

Beth I. aged 9

Q. What kind of shoes do lawyers wear?

A. Court shoes

Elizabeth O. aged 9

Q. What shoes should you wear when your house floods?

A. Pumps

Michael J. aged 10

Q. What did the shoes say to the socks?

A. You're putting me on

Jonas P. aged 8

Animal Attraction

**Elephants on marshmallows
Always get a reaction
But pigs and dogs and zebras
Have Animal Attraction**

Q. Why did the elephant sit on the marshmallow?

A. To stop itself falling in the hot chocolate

Fiona L. aged 4

Q. What's black, white and blue?

A. A zebra at the North Pole   Chris B. aged 10

Q. How do you take a pig to hospital?

A. In a Hambulance   Deni R. aged 10

Q. How do you stop a dog from barking?

A. Put it in a barking lot   Zoe T. aged 6

Q. What is a horse's favourite T.V. show?

A. Neighbours

Hannah P. aged 10

Q. Why was the crab arrested?

A. Because he kept pinching things   Sophie D. aged 7

Andy's Aunties' Funky

Forget-Me-Nots

**P.S. These jokes have been endorsed by
1,000,000,000,000,000 Aunts! Hello!**

Q. What do you call a Bavarian rash?

A. A German measle

Cassie L. aged 10

Q. What do you call a pig in a restaurant?

A. A pig out

Walter K. aged 6

Q. Why did the runner wear rippled soled shoes?

A. To give the ants a 50/50 chance   Craig G. aged 7

Q. What type of shellfish lift heavy weights?

A. Mussells

Kris L. aged 10

A bit of this
And that, my friends
A funny lot of
Odds 'n' Ends

Q. Who's your best friend at school?

A. **Your Princi-pal**   Stacey J. aged 9

Q. What did the hat say to the scarf?

A. **You hang around and I'll go ahead**   Nick B. aged 9

Q. What are hundreds and thousands?

A. **Smarty droppings** Caris B. aged 10

Q. What sort of vegetables do athletes prefer?

A. **Runner beans**
Marnie B. aged 8

Q. Who is the best
underwater spy?

A. **James Pond**
Ben J. aged 10

Q. Why shouldn't you
tell secrets to a clock?

A. **Because time will always tell** Alex H. aged 10

Q. What did the dentist say to his wife when she baked
a cake?

A. **Can I do the filling?** Charlee C. aged 8

Q. Why was Mr Maths upset?

A. Because his son was a problem Amber C. aged 12

Q. Why was Cinderella thrown off the netball team?

A. Because she kept running away from the ball
Mathew R. aged 11

Animal
Magnetism

They're regal, majestic
And love to run free
Animal Magnetism
Is something to see

Q. What do you get if you cross a mouse with a pip?

A. **A pip-squeak** Natasha. S. aged 10

Q. What do sheep eat?

A. **Chocolate baas** Fiona F. aged 11

Q. What do you call a sheep in a bikini?

A. **Bra Bra Black Sheep** Joel G. aged 6

Q. Why couldn't the pony talk?

A. **'Cause he was a little horse** Nelly N. aged 6

Q. What do geese do in traffic jams?

A. **They honk**
Keely R.R. aged 12

194

Q. What do you call a woodpecker without a beak?

A. A head banger Marli H. aged 10

Q. What do you call a bunch of tweety birds?

A. A squawkestra Kelly P. aged 8

Q. Where do rabbits go when they get married?

A. On a bunny moon Sarah D. aged 6

Q. What do you get when you walk under a cow?

A. A pat on the head
Renee W. aged 12

Q. What do you get when you tickle a cow?

A. A good kick out of it Lynette A. aged 10

Q. What do you call a cow that eats grass?

A. **A lawn mooer**   Leathan S. aged 7

Q. How does a farmer count his cows?

A. **With a cowculator**   Louise J. aged 8

Q. Did you hear about the Frenchman who hated snails?

A. **He liked fast food**
James M. aged 9

Q. Why did the bees go on strike?

A. **They wanted shorter flowers and more honey**
Kerry R. aged 10

Q. How do fish go into business?

A. **They start small-scale**
Geoffrey A.R. aged 11

Q. What type of fur do you get from a brown bear?

A. **As fur away as possible** Lathan W. aged 6

Q. What do you call a white bear who loves to lie in the sun listening to pop music, rolling balls and drinking soft drink?

A. **A solar, roller, bowler, cola-polar**
Felicity W. aged 11

Q. What do you get if you cross a hyena with a shark?

A. **I don't know, but if it laughs I'll join in**
Randall S. aged 6

Q. What did the dinosaur say when it saw the volcano erupt?

A. What a lava-ly day

Daniel E. aged 10

Batty Blunders

Moonlit nights
And cracking thunder
Vampire jokes and
Batty Blunders

Q. Why is it easy to trick a vampire?

A. **Because they're all suckers**   Robbie S. aged 7

Q. What do you call a vampire's dog?

A. **A blood hound** Ashley D. aged 9

Q. What do vampires use to catch fish?

A. **Bloodworms** Kevin C. aged 12

Q. What kind of ships do vampires sail?

A. **Blood vessels** Greta P. aged 6

Q. What happens when you upset a vampire?

A. He sees red Arnold J. aged 11

Q. What type of girls do vampires like?

A. Red heads Tricia M. aged 6

Q. What do you call vampire twins?

A. Blood brothers Kevin C. aged 12

Q. Where do vampires go for holidays?

A. Batavia Collin P. aged 12

Q. What do vampires bath in?

A. A bloodbath Terri W. aged 8

Q. When is a vampire a super hero?

A. When he's Batman
Allicia C. aged 7

Star Struck

They shoot through the sky
So get ready to duck
If you gaze too deeply
You'll become Star Struck!

Q. What sort of star is dangerous?

A. **A shooting star**

Maree D. aged 9

Q. What do you call a famous rock?

A. **A rock star**

Kent B. aged 10

Q. What do you call a young star?

A. **A grommit-comet**
Dale S. aged 10

Q. How do you get a baby astronaut to sleep?

A. **Rocket**
Chloe M.D. aged 10

Q. What happened to the two planets that collided?

A. **They were star-tled**
Virginia Q. aged 11

Q. What do you call an intergalactic garbage truck?

A. **A dump-star**
Angelo M. aged 10

Q. What star only comes out on Mondays?

A. **A mon-star** Nick Joseph aged 35, Jacaranda Retirement Home

Q. What do you call the referee at a cosmic athletics meeting?

A. **The star-ter** Angela L. aged 12

Q. What did the alien say to the plant?

A. **Take me to your weeder** Carl K. aged 9

bananarama

They're bright and yellow
And nothing like llamas
We all eat them
They're called Bananas

Q. What do you say to a frozen banana?

A. Cool banana   Lisa R. aged 11

Q. What do you call a sunburnt banana?

A A banana peel   Genna S. aged 8

Q. What do
bananas
wear for
underwear?

**A. I don't know,
peel one
and see**
Kelvin J.
aged 10

Q. Why is a banana skin like a T-shirt?

A. Because it's easy to slip on
Marnie B. aged 8

Q. What do you call a sheep that eats bananas?

A. A Baa-Baa-nana
Andrew P. aged 9

Can-tankerous

Some hold spaghetti
Some hold ham
There's nothing quite like
The humble tin can!

Q. What's a can's favourite card game?

A. **Canasta**
Lenny P. aged 9

Q. What's yellow, made of steel and can fly?

A. **A canary**
Courtney L. aged 9

Q. What's a can's favourite dance?

A. **The Can Can**
Trent T. aged 8

Q. What's a can's best friend?

A. **Rin Tin Tin**
Lenny P. aged 9

Q. What do you get if you cross a can with a poodle?

A. **A can-noodle**
Trent T. aged 8

Q. What's a can's favourite music?

A. **Heavy metal**
Lilly A. aged 8

Q. What do you call a can with a sweet tooth?

A. **Candy**
John H. aged 8

Q. When is a can not a can?

A. **When it's uncanny**
Allivia S. aged 5

Q. Where do cans go for their holidays?

A. **Canada**
Eva H. aged 8

Q. What do you call a can that takes pictures?

A. **A handy-can**
Ellen G. aged 9

Q. What do you get if you cross a bird with a can?

A. **A tou-can**
Elliot W. aged 8

It's not ham and eggs
Or bacon from porkers
It's a whole
new section
Of roaring Ripsnorters!

rip**snor**ters

Q. How do pigs get to hospital?

A. **In a hambulance**

Greg P. aged 6

Q. What do you call a greedy pig?

A. **A hog**

Allan T. aged 7

To eat or not to eat? That is the question. Whether 'tis nobler for the swine...

Q. What do you call a theatrical pig?

A. **Hamlet**
Mark A. aged 8

Q. Where do pigs go for their holidays?

A. **Hamsterdam**
Mary W. aged 7

Q. What's a pig's favourite sport?

A. **Hamball**
Melanie F. aged 8

Q. What does a pig call his grandfather?

A **Hampa**
Tristen G. aged 6

Q. What do pigs call second-hand clothes?

A. **Ham-me-downs**
Petra T. aged 7

Terrific Tomatoes

They're red and juicy
They squirt up your nose!
Those squishy, delishy
Terrific Tomatoes

Q. What's red, round and juicy, and has toes but no feet?

A. **Tomatoes**
Caplan W. aged 10

Q. What did the police do to the suspicious tomato?

A. **They grilled him** Simon R. aged 7

Q. When does a tomato become another vegetable?

A. When it gets squashed   Mavis B. aged 9

Q. What's better than one tomato?

A. To-matoes   Nick L. aged 8

Q. What do you call a sunburnt potato?

A. A tomato   Gill G. aged 9

I Knew That

They always say it
Right off the bat
"I told you so"
"I knew that"

Q. Why did the toilet paper roll down the hill?

A. **To get to the bottom**   Bradley M. aged 9

Q. Where does a snowman dance?

A. **At a snow ball**   Kasey O. aged 11

Q. What do you call a pair of underwear thieves?

A. **A pair of knickers!**   Kylie V. aged 8

Q. What sort of biscuits can fly?

A. **Plain biscuits**
Jessica M. aged 1

Q. What gets bigger the more you take away?

A. **A hole**   Matthew T. aged 8

Q. What kind of pliers do you use in maths?

A. **Multipliers**   Erica T. aged 11

Q. What gets wet as it dries?

A. **A towel**   Michelle J. aged 9

Q. Why did the girl throw her toast out of the window?

A. **She wanted to see the butterfly**
Ashlee R. aged 10

Q. What three letters are robbers scared of?

A. **I.C.U.** Regina W. aged 9

Q. Why was Isaac Newton, the mathematics genius, surprised when he was hit on the head by an apple?

A. **He was sitting under a pear tree** Janelle P. aged 11

Q. What banks never run out of money?

A. **River banks** Rebecca G. aged 12

Q. What happened to the man that sat on the pin?

A. **He got the point** Rebecca G. aged 12

Q. What do you call a boomerang that doesn't come back?

A. **A stick**
Samuel S. aged 10

Q. Did you get the joke about the sun?

A. **No, I didn't, it was above my head**
Rebecca S. aged 10

Q. What do you call a goat with small knees?

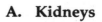

A. **Kidneys**
Scott P. aged 9

Q. How many birthdays have you had?

A. **One, because you're only born once**
Lesley E. aged 11

Q. What did one candle say to the other candle?

A. **I'm going out tonight**
Jack M. aged 10

Q. Where do you find lots of keys that don't open anything?

A. **On a piano**
Mitchell J. aged 9

Q. How do you talk to a giant?

A. **You use big words**
Glen F. aged 7

Monday to Sunday

Each day is

an adventure

Each day is a fun day

So keep on laughing

From Monday to Sunday!

Q. What's the most
boring day?

A. **Mun-day**
Aedan P. aged 10

Q. What's the best day to
decide what to wear?

A. **Choose-day**
Kelly S. aged 12

Q. What's the best day to get married?

A. **Wed-nesday** Vanessa A. aged 12

Q What's the best day to drink orange juice?

A. **Thirst-day** Candice M. aged 12

Q. What is the best day to eat bacon and eggs?

A. **Fry-day** Wendy P. aged 12

Q. What's the best day to lounge around?

A. **Sat-urday** Lucille S.P. aged 12

Q. What's the best day for fathers and sons to get together?

A. **Son-day** Frank L. aged 12

Knock
Knock

There's a knock
on the door
And an answer — who's there?
It's bound to be funny —
Read on — if you dare!

Knock Knock

Who's there?

Oh no

Oh no who?

Oh no, I've got the wrong house

Sharnee B. aged 8

Knock Knock

Who's there?

Scott

Scott who?

Scott nothing to do with you

Kelvin H. aged 8

Knock Knock

Who's there?

Shirley

Shirley who?

Shirley I don't need to tell you

Fiona F. aged 10

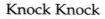

Knock Knock

Who's there?

Who

Who who?

Are you an owl?

Dane T. aged 8

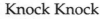

Knock Knock

Who's there?

Freeze

Freeze who?

Freeze a jolly good fellow

Peter G. aged 10

Knock Knock

Who's there?

Little old lady

Little old lady who?

I never knew you could yodel

Luke T. aged 9

Knock Knock

Who's there?

Theresa

Theresa who?

Theresa green

Jacob G. aged 10

Knock Knock

Who's there?

Omer

Omer who?

Omer goodness wrong door

Amber M. aged 9

Knock Knock

Who's there?

Mice

Mice who?

Mice to meet you

Nathan J. aged 8

Knock Knock

Who's there?

Cook

Cook who?

**That's the first
one I've heard this year**   Fiona F. aged 10

Knock Knock

Who's there?

Amanda

Amanda who?

Amanda fix the TV

Ashton W. aged 11

Knock Knock

Who's there?

Ashley

Ashley who?

Ashley I want to play cards

Shannon B. aged 11

Knock Knock

Who's there?

Bok! Bok!

Bok! Bok! who?

Bok! Bok! I'm a chicken

Cassie W. aged 10

Knock Knock

Who's there?

Irish stew

Irish stew who?

Irish stew in the name of the law

Hope M. aged 12

Knock Knock

Who's there?

Abby

Abby who?

Abby Birthday

Melissa P. aged 10

Knock Knock

Who's there?

Iva

Iva who?

Iva sore hand from knocking on the door   Hayley N. aged 9

225

Funky
Monkeys

They hang from trees
And look real spunky
Those playful primates
The Funky Monkeys!

Q. Where do monkeys cook their toast?

A. **Under the gorilla**
Brodie T. aged 8

Q. What do you get if you cross a gorilla and a skunk?

A. **King Pong**
Scott G. aged 11

Q. What do you call a 2000 pound gorilla?

A. **Sir**
Dwayne S. aged 10

Q. Where do baby apes sleep?

A. **In apricots**
Brodie T. aged 10

226

Q. What do you call a gorilla with custard in one ear and jelly in the other?

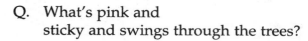

A. **Anything you want, it can't hear you**
Nicola V.B. aged 10

Q. What's pink and sticky and swings through the trees?

A. **A merangutan**   Joneen G. aged 11

Q. Why do gorillas have big fingers?

A. **Because they have big nostrils**   Sara B. aged 11

Furniture
Follies

Look around the lounge room
And you'll get the jollies
The decor is funky
It's the Furniture Follies!

Q. What rocks and rolls but can't dance?

A. **A washing machine**   Kitty K. aged 7

Q. What's Elvis Presley's favourite seat?

A. **A rockin' chair**   Ellis S. aged 7

Q. What's the brightest baby in the house?

A. **A light bub**   Amity V. aged 11

Q. What sort of table can you drink?

A. **A coffee table**   Kelly P. aged 8

Q. What kind of furniture can you eat?

A. **Lounge sweets**
Becky F.
aged 8

Pretty
Kitty

Feline purring makes
Moggy ditties
Whiskers and milk
For Pretty Kitties

Q. What can cats have that dogs can't?

A. Kittens   Lauren W. aged 9

Q. What do you call a cat with no legs?

A. Anything you like, it won't come anyway
                                                       Natasha S. aged 12

Q. What is a cat's favourite sport?

A. Puss-ups   Kieren M. aged 6

Q. What do you get if you cross a cat with a grub?

A. A caterpillar   Renee G. aged 7

Q. What do you call a messy cat?

A. Kitty Litter Debra D. aged 8

Q. Why did the cat join St John's Ambulance?

A. It wanted to be a first aid kit Daniella O. aged 7

Q. Why are cats afraid to go outside?

A. 'Cause they're scaredy cats Maddison T. aged 6

Q. Where do you find a new cat?

A. In a catalogue Stacey S. aged 8

Brain
Benders

Let's all share the pain
We're all mental members
Of the Kool Klub
The Incredible Brain Benders

Q. What do you call a bee born in May?

A. A May-bee   Claudia M. aged 6

Q. What has fingers but can't play the piano?

A. A glove   Rhia S. aged 9

Q. Why were there only 24 letters in the alphabet?

A. Because U and I weren't there   Hayley B. aged 12

Q. What do you do if you want to double your money?

A. Fold it in half
Lynette A. aged 10

Q. What did the biscuit say when another biscuit got run over by a car?

A. **Crumbs!** Jess M. aged 11

Q. How many sides does a circle have?

A. **Two — one on the inside and one on the outside!**
Brayden P. aged 9

Q. What has three eyes and one leg?

A. **Traffic lights** Brodie T. aged 10

They fly around
And annoy you lots
The time has come
For Fly Swats!

Q. What did the fly say when he hit the window?

A. If I had the guts I'd do that again Chris P. aged 12

Q. Where do flies do their shopping?

A. Where they can get Fly Buys Selwyn B. aged 12

Q. What do you call a fly without wings?

A. A walk Jason A. aged 6

Q. Why did the fly fall off the wall?

A. Because he had a fridge tied to his leg

Damon B. aged 10

Twisted Tunes

You can sing to your budgie
You can sing to the moon
There's nothing like singing
The odd Twisted Tune

Q. What is a ram's favourite song?

A. **I'll Never Find Another Ewe**

Donna M. aged 9

Q. What type of
pet has no
eyes, legs and
you never have
to feed it?

A. **A trumpet**
Grace M. aged 11

Q. What's a heart's favourite song?

A. **The Beat Goes On**
Cassie P. aged 10

Q. What's a zebra's favourite song?

A. **The Lion Sleeps Tonight**
Anthony K. aged 9

Q. What type of phone never rings?

A. **A saxa-phone**
Kendall M. aged 7

Q. What is a pig's favourite instrument?

A. **A tam-boar-ine!**
Lenard Q. aged 9

One must ask
What's in a name?
Let's all play ...

The Name Game

Q. What do you call a man who grows herbs?

A. **Herbert**
Ellenor D. aged 9

Q. What do you call a man who likes fishing?

A. **Rod**
Reggie B. aged 12

Q. What do you call a woman who hangs out the washing?

A. **Peg**   Zane H. aged 12

Q. What do you call a man who likes the sun?

A. **Ray**   Ravi L. aged 10

Q. What do you call a woman who likes butter?

A. **Marj**   Francis F. aged 8

Q. What do you call a girl that likes jewellery?

A. **Jules**
Chris D. aged 10

Q. What do you call a woman who gets up early?

A. **Dawn**
Catherine B.M. aged 12

Q. What do you call a woman who mends fences?

A. **Barb**   Melanie L. aged 7

Q. What do you call a man with a car on his head?

A. **Jack**   Rebecca M. aged 10

Don't try this at home kids

Q. What do you call a girl with a frog on her head?

A. **Lilly**   Bree C. aged 9

Q. What do you call a woman who's good at saving money?

A. **Penny**   Stephen F. aged 10

Q. What do you call a girl traffic light?

A. **Amber**   Julie N.P. aged 6

Q. What do you call a man with a shovel?

A. **Doug**   Lorryndle E. aged 12

Traffic

Jams

Q. What kind of discos do traffic lights go to?

A. **Green light discos**
Abelle P. aged 11

Q. What's sweet and sticky and stops traffic?

A. **A traffic jam**
Justin R. aged 7

Q. Why did the chicken cross the road carrying a pair of scissors?

A. **Because he wanted to cut corners**   Michelle D. aged 10

Q. What's an intersection's favourite ride?

A. **A roundabout**   Lucy D. aged 12

Q. When do you get that run down feeling?

A. **When you've been hit by a truck** Ryan G. aged 8

Q. Why did the computer cross the road?

A. **The chook programmed it**
Chris P. aged 12

They bark and ruff
And don't like moggies
Those canine jokers
The Dinky Doggies

Dinky DOGgies

Q. What did the dog say when it sat on some sandpaper?

A. **Ruff Ruff**

Jade L. aged 12

Q. What do you call a dog that sits in the sun?

A. **A hot dog**

Chris K. aged 9

Q. What do you get if you cross a mutt with a poodle?

A. **A muddle**
Derek T. aged 8

Q. How does a hunter find his lost dog?

A. **He puts his ear to a tree and listens to the bark**
Adam T. aged 10

Q. What did the
   dog say
   when he
   burnt his
   tail?

A. **This is the
   end of me**
   Amanda T. aged 10

Q. What do you get when you cross a skunk and a
   poodle?

A. **A smelly dog**   Emma R. aged 8

Q. What do you call a spaced-out dog?

A. **A pluto pup**   Amanda B. aged 8

Q. What do you call a poodle that can ski?

A. **A ski-doodle**   Kell R. aged 12

Ant-itude

In families of millions
It's hard to find food
For six-legged insects
With Ant-itude

Q. What do you call a really smart ant?

A. Stud-ant
Rachel P. aged 11

Q. Where do ants go for their holidays?

A. Ant-arctica
Bianca P. aged 10

Q. What do you call an ant in the army?

A. Sergeant
Debbie P. aged 9

Q. What do ants study at university?

A. Ant-atomy
Katrina B. aged 9

Q. What do you call
a really fat ant?

A. **An elephant**
Karen K. aged 10

Q. What do you call
an ant that won't
move?

A. **Stagnant**
Peter G. aged 9

Q. What's a really
happy ant?

A. **Exhuber-ant**
Josephine M. aged 8

Q. What sort of ant lives on your TV?

A **An antenna**   Mark A. aged 8

Q. What are the biggest ants in the world?

A. **Elephants!**   Kerry B. aged 6

Excellent Elephants

Why did the elephant Cross the road with the chook? To read all the jokes In this red hot book!

Q. What is grey, big and beautiful?

A. **Cinderelephant**   Samantha K. aged 10

Q. What did the elephant pack his clothes in?

A. **His trunk**   Janelle F.
aged 5

Q. What do you get if you cross an elephant with a computer?

A. **A two-tonne know it all**
Michael L.M. aged 11

Q. Why are elephants wrinkled?

A. **Have you ever tried ironing one?**
Rhianna C. aged 10

Q. What do you give a sea-sick elephant?

A. **Lots of room**   Mitchell J. aged 9

Andy's Hot Shots

They're Hot and Kool
And always hit the spot
Andy's funky favourites
Super-Kool-Hot-Shots!

Q.   What is the Funky Monkey's favourite TV show?

A.   The Groovy Moovy!   Kaedyn H. aged 10

A schoolboy went to the teacher and said, "May I go to the bathroom?" The teacher answered, "First say the alphabet", so he started saying it:

"ABCDEFGHIJKLMNOQRSTUVWXYZ".

When the boy had finished the teacher asked, "What happened to the P?"

The boy looked down.

Caris M. aged 11

A man walked into a shop and asked for a fork. He got one.

Another man walked in and asked for a fork. He got one.

Then another man walked in and asked for a fork. He got one too.

Then another man walked in and asked for a straw.

"Why do you want a straw when everyone else wants a fork?"

The man answered, "Someone threw up on the sidewalk and all the chunky bits are gone."

Lauren M. aged 12

Jack: "I wish I had enough money to buy an elephant."

Jill: "Why do you want to buy an elephant?"

Jack: "I don't, I just wish I had the money."

Dylan O. aged 8

There were two men out fishing. Both were old and had false teeth. One man said to the other, "Oh no! I've lost my false teeth."

The other man thought this was funny and decided to play a trick on his friend, so he took his false teeth out and put them on the end of his fishing line and said to the other man, "Hey, look — I've caught your teeth on my line."

So the man who lost his teeth looked at them and said, "No, they're not my teeth" and threw them back in the water!

Tim S. aged 11

A flea walked into a milkbar, drank a milkshake and then walked out. Soon after he came back in.

"I thought you'd left," said the woman behind the counter.

The flea replied, "I did, but someone stole my dog!"

Natasha S. aged 12

A man was walking down a street with a penguin and a policeman came up and said, "Why don't you take that penguin to the zoo!" The man said, "What a good idea." The next day he was walking down the road with the penguin and the policeman came up and said, "I thought I told you to take that penguin to the zoo." The man said, "I did, and today I'm taking him to the movies!"

Regina W. aged 12

Sales Rep: "I keep logs on my travels."

Friend: "Oh really. I don't keep logs, I make them into furniture."

Simon C. aged 11

Son: "Dad, Dad, I came top in arithmetic today! The teacher asked what 3x15 was and I answered 42."

Father: "But that's wrong, the answer is 45."

Son: "I know, but I was closer than anyone else!"

Fiona F. aged 10

Andy's Top Ten

Words of wisdom
From young women and men
Best of the best
It's Andy's Top Ten

Q Why couldn't James make an ice cube?

A **Because he didn't know the recipe**   Elli I. aged 7

Mother: "What is the difference between an elephant's trunk and a postbox?"

Son: "I don't know."

Mother: "I won't send YOU to post my letters."

Marc A. aged 10

Q How do you kiss a hockey player?

A **You puck-er up**
Claire L. aged 9

Q Why is milk so fast?

A **Because it's pasteurised before you see it**

Emma X. aged 10

251

Q   What happens if your nose runs and your feet smell?

A   **You've been turned upside down**
Claire L. aged 9

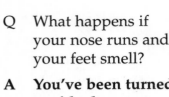

Q   What happened to the boy who drank nine cokes?

A   **He burped 7 up**
Jayden L. aged 8

Girl: "Are they braces you're wearing?"

Boy: "No, it's just a muzzle that keeps me from biting people who ask stupid questions."
Claudia L. aged 10

Q   What has limbs but can't walk?

A   **A tree**
Catiline M. aged 6

Q   What happens when you go bald?

A   **You have to carry your dandruff in your pocket**
Brian P. aged 8

Q   What's green and eats porridge?

A   **Mouldilocks**
Marc A. aged 10

Fly-Bye-Byes

It's jumbo jets and
Friendly skies
Let's take off with
Fly-Bye-Byes

Q How does an airline pilot's child say goodnight?

A **Goodnight Mummy, goodnight Daddy — over and out!**
Elizabeth S. aged 7

Q What is big, hairy and can fly?

A **King-Kong-corde**
Penelope F. aged 9

Q Why did the flying angel lose his job?

A **Because he had harp failure**
Hanson T. aged 10

Q What kind of dog can catch a plane?

A **A jet setter**
Mana F. aged 7

Q Where do birds invest their money?

A **In the stork market**
Sascha L. aged 6

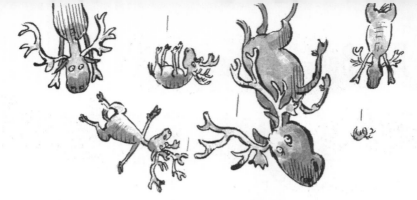

Q   What animal drops from the clouds?

A   **A raindeer**   Joe Q. aged 8

Q   What do planes wear on their engines to keep them warm?

A   **Jet-warmers**   Leigh B. aged 8

Q   What do you call a plane that flies from point A to point B then back to point A?

A   **A double crosser**   Lisa Y. aged 9

Q   Why are planes good mimics?

A   **Because they do great take offs**   Madlyn L. aged 7

Q   Where do roosters go when they get to the airport?

A   **The chick-in**   Lizzie C. aged 9

Q   What happens if pigs fly?

A   **Bacon goes up**   Seamus G. aged 9

Q   What is the nicest plane in the world?

A   **A Fokker Friendship**   Ryan S. aged 6

Q   What do you call a plane that talks a lot?

A   **A mumbo jumbo**   Huon F. aged 7

Q   What is a rooster's favourite part of a plane?

A   **The cock-pit**   Andy N. aged 9

Q   What has two wings it can't flap, a beak it can't eat
    with and no feathers but can fly?

A   **An aeroplane**   Nigel L. aged 10

Q   What type of plane does E.T. fly on?

A   **A jE.T.**   Dylan S. aged 9

Q What do you call a plane that fails to fly?

A **An aero-flop** Sandra P. aged 8

Q How do bank robbers escape by air?

A **They make a quick jetaway** Pauline W. aged 9

Q What do pilots do when they're bored?

A **Play aeronauts and crosses** Diana P. aged 7

Q How do you know when a pilot has a tummy upset?

A **He gets burpulence** Tim T. aged 6

Q Where do pilots go fishing?

A **In the jet stream** Tegan R. aged 9

Passenger: "I hope this plane doesn't travel faster than the speed of sound."
Flight attendant: "Why?"
Passenger: "Because my friend and I want to talk." Gillian T. aged 10

Body Parts

Double chins
And beating hearts
Piece 'em together
Body Parts

Q   Why did the lady put lipstick on her head?

A   **Because she wanted to make-up her mind**   Gabriella B. aged 10

Q   What do you call a sticky knee?

A   **Hon-ey**   Liam F. aged 5

Q   What type of knee can you get at a bank?

A   **Mon-ey**   Ben H. aged 5

Q   What do you call a knee which tells jokes?

A   **Fun-ny**   Madeleine L. aged 10

Q   What type of room can you fit in your mouth?

A   **A mushroom**   Daniel S. aged 8

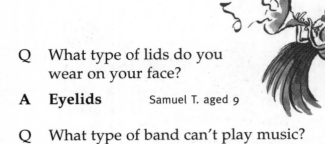

Q   What type of lids do you wear on your face?

A   **Eyelids**   Samuel T. aged 9

Q   What type of band can't play music?

A   **A hair band**   Prashad T. aged 8

Q   What type of stick can you put on your face?

A   **Lipstick**   Genevieve K. aged 7

Q   What do you call a baby knee?

A   **A mini**   Rhiannon L. aged 7

Q   What type of cage has no bars?

A   **A rib cage**   Joanne S. aged 9

Q   What do you call beautiful hands?

A   **Hand-some**   Kayla S. aged 8

Q   Where do arms like to sit?

A   **In an armchair**   Rory F. aged 6

Q   What type of ribbon lives on your arm?

A   **An el-bow**   Tania B. aged 9

Q   What do you call a sleepy head?

A   **A bed-head**   Tania B. aged 9

Sizzling Hot Shots

Pots and cots
Knots and tots
Lots and lots of
Sizzling Hot Shots

Q   What has a neck but no head?

A   **A bottle**   Vanessa T. aged 11

Q   Why is a rabbit's nose always shiny?

A   **Because the powder puff is at the wrong end**   Lauren A. aged 7

Q   What nut sounds like a sneeze?

A   **A cashew**   Pepe S. aged 6

Q   What is a complete waste of time?

A   **Telling a hair-raising story to a bald man**

Daniel F. aged 10

Q   Where do sheep cook their meat?

A   **On a Baa-b-que**

Mitchell H. aged 10

Q   If two's company and
    three's a crowd, what
    are four and five?

A   **Nine**
    Louis B. aged 6

Q   Why is tennis a noisy
    game?

A   **When you play it you
    have to raise a racket**
    Jessica B. aged 6

Q   What runs but has
    no legs?

A   **A tap**
    Hayden T. aged 8

Q   What did the farmer
    say when he saw
    his cow in a tree?

A   **"Get down!"**
    Stephanie L. aged 9

Keys Please

There's lots of fun
In riddles like these
But they're hard to unravel
Pass the Keys Please!

Q   What type of key can you wipe your nose with?

A   **A han-key**   Matthew S. aged 9

Q   What do you call a beautiful key?

A   **Spun-key**   Elizabeth P. aged 10

Q   What do you call a long key?

A   **Lan-key**   Shelley K. aged 7

Q   What do you call a grumpy key?

A   **Sul-key**   Kristina R. aged 9

Q   What do you call a key that wins you money?

A   **Luc-key**

Ariadne A. aged 6

Q   What do you call an angry key?

A   **Cran-key**

Genevieve M. aged 9

Q   What sort of food do keys eat?

A   **Bic-keys**

Helena B. aged 9

Q   What do you call a key in a leather jacket?

A   **A bi-key**

James E. aged 6

Q   What country do keys come from?

A   **Tur-key**   Luke S. aged 7

Q   What does a key wear to the beach?

A   **A bi-key-ni**   Ryan T. aged 8

African Animals

Hanging from trees
Dining with cannibals
They're so exotic
African Animals

Q   What do you call a rhinoceros who swings through the trees?

A   **A vinoceros**
    Susan S. aged 7

Q   Why does a giraffe have a long neck?

A   **Because he can't stand the smell of his feet**
    Casey C. aged 7

Q   Where did Tarzan buy his clothes?

A   **At a jungle sale**   Jane S. aged 7

Q   What kind of monkey can fly?

A   **A hot air baboon**   Dean T. aged 8

Q   What is pretty, has big teeth and flies?

A   **A killer butterfly**   Joe S. aged 8

Q   Why couldn't the leopard escape from the zoo?

A   **Because he was always spotted**   Adam J. aged 9

Q   What is hairy and coughs?

A   **A coconut with a cold**
Benjamin S. aged 9

Q   What do cannibals have for lunch?

A   **Baked beings**   Kayleigh C. aged 8

Q   What should you do for a starving cannibal?

A   **Give him a hand**   Vicki W. aged 7

Q   What do cannibals eat for breakfast?

A   **Buttered host**   Chamberlain Y. aged 8

Q   What do you call a really messy hippo?

A   **A hippopota-mess**   James J. aged 10

Q   What's the largest mouse in the world?

A   **A hippopota-mouse**

Lydia T. aged 7

267

Q Which animal is always laughing?

A **A happy-potamus**   Jane R. aged 7

Q What do you call an out-of-breath mammoth?

A **An ele-pant**   Caren R. aged 6

Q What's tall and smells nice?

A **A Giraff-o-dill**   Shani R. aged 7

Q What is striped and goes around and around?

A **A zebra in a revolving door**   Anna S. aged 9

Q What swings through the trees and is very dangerous?

A **A chimpanzee with a machine gun**
Vince S. aged 10

What a Load of Croc!

Menacing reptiles
And jaws that lock
Gnawing of funny bones
What a Load of Croc!

Q How do you phone up a croc?

A **You croc-a-dial**
Chris A. aged 9

Q What do you get if you cross a rooster with a crocodile?

A **A croc-a-doodle-doo**
Joanna H. aged 10

Q What time is it when you meet a crocodile?

A **Time to run**
Freya O. aged 9

Q   What do crocodiles cook their food in?

A   **Croc pots**   Ingrid M. aged 7

Q   What do you call a crocodile that goes door to door?

A   **A sales rep-tile**   Andrew M. aged 10

Computer Chips

Games and screensavers
And electronic blips
They all run on
Computer Chips

Q   Where do computers go to dance?

A   **The disk-o**   Michael O. aged 8

Q   When is a key-bored?

A   **When it is with a computer**   Thomas P. aged 8

Q   What is a computer's favourite animal?

A   **A mouse**   James P. aged 10

Q   What do all computers look through?

A   **Windows**   Troy R. aged 8

Q   What do you call a high-voltage computer?

A   **An AC-DC PC**   Brent O. aged 10

Q   How do computers catch fish?

A   **In-ter-net**   Matthew O. aged 10

Q   How do you know when a computer wants to stay over?

A   **It wants to DOS**   Adrian M. aged 10

Q   What's the difference between a boxer and a computer?

A   **You only need to punch information into a computer once**   Benjamin K. aged 9

Q   How do you know when a computer is tired?

A   **It takes floppy disks**
Jessica R. aged 6

Q   What do you get when you cross 2000 smarties and a computer?

A   **A multi-coloured smarty party**   Danielle K. aged 8

Q   How do computers go through a divorce?

A   **They Control-Alt-Delete**   Jenna S. aged 10

Q   What do you call a gorgeous computer?

A   **A QT PC**   Brittany C. aged 10

Songs of the Sea

Listen up me hearties
Wherever you be
To these wet and wild
Songs of the Sea

Q   What does a deaf fisherman need?

A   **A herring aide**   Margaret W. aged 9

Q   What kind of cat lives in the ocean?

A   **An octo-pus**   Jack B. aged 7

Q   How do you make a goldfish old?

A   **Take away the G**   Robert D. aged 7

Q   What do you call a really quiet fish?

A   **A shh…shh…shark**   Nicola R. aged 8

Q   Where do dead fish swim?

A   **In the Dead Sea**   Suzie S. aged 9

Q   Where do seagulls rest at sea?

A   **On a perch**   Matt C. aged 6

Q   What type of fish is best eaten at the beginning of
     the week?

A   **Barra-Monday**   Mane C. aged 7

Q What do you call an angry fish?

A **Snapper** Nicholas E. aged 9

Q What do you get if you jump in the Red Sea?

A **Wet** Lucas B. aged 9

Q How do you make a sea creature rich?

A **Take the S out of squid — quid** Ciara C. aged 8

Q What did one rockpool say to the other?

A **Show us your mussels** Matthew C. aged 7

Q What dives under the sea and carries 64 people?

A **An octo-bus** Justin R. aged 7

Q What do you call a baby whale?

A **A little squirt** Christopher M. aged 9

Q What is a shark's favourite vegetable?

A **A crab-bage**

Kristina B. aged 9

Q What do you call a sea mammal in pain?

A **A squeal**

Michael L. aged 10

Q What do mermaids eat for breakfast?

A **Mermalade on toast**

Emma P. aged 6

Feathered Funnies

They're not clucking horses
Or quacking bunnies
But they tweet and they crow
They're the Feathered Funnies

Q   What do ducks watch on TV?

A   Duckumentaries   Ashleigh R. aged 8

Q   What goes cluck cluck bang?

A   A chicken in a minefield   Timothy M. aged 7

Q   What did the magpie say to the scarecrow?

A   I'll knock the stuffing out of you   Nathan S. aged 9

Q What is the most common illness in birds?

A **Flu** William T. aged 7

Q Why does Batman look for worms?

A **To feed his Robin** Julian P. aged 8

Q What bird is always laughing?

A **A kooky-burra** Adam W. aged 6

Q What did the owl say after the square dance?

A **That was a hoot** Laura N. aged 7

Q When is the best time to buy budgies?

A **When they are going cheep** Denis A. aged 11

Q What do you get if you cross a bird with a fly?

A **A fly-fly** Holly J. aged 6

Q   What do chickens expect at the theatre?

A   **Hentertainment**   Martin B. aged 8

Q   How did the exhausted sparrow land safely?

A   **By sparrow-chute**   Jack J. aged 7

Q   What are feathers good for?

A   **Birds**   April F. aged 9

Q Where do sparrows go on holidays?

A **Sparrow-dice**   Sam Q. aged 7

Q How do sparrows tell the future?

A **Sparrow cards**   Lisa F. aged 10

Q What do you get if
   you run over a
   sparrow with a lawn
   mower?

A **Shredded tweet**

Jordan D. aged 7

Q What do you call a pig
   that flies?

A **A pig-eon**   Margi R. aged 9

Q What kind of
   pie can fly?

A **A magpie**

Michelle S.
aged 7

Miraculous Mothers

A reassuring hug
That's better than all others
They're the best
Miraculous Mothers

Q What's a mother's favourite jam?

A **Mama-lade**   Holly F. aged 6

Q What do you get if you cross a mother with a lot of humps?

A **Mumps**   Caitlin L. aged 7

Q What do you call a big mum?

A **Maxi-mum**   Andrew E. aged 8

Q What do you call a little mum?

A **Mini-mum**   Andrew E. aged 8

Q   What did the hungry shark say when he saw a mother swimming?

A   **Mmm... A yummy mummy**   Samuel S. aged 8

Q   What do you call a mummy who sings in the shower?

A   **A hummy**   Isaac L. aged 9

Q   What do you call a mother with bread on her lap?

A   **A crumby mummy**   Jessica B. aged 6

Q   What does your mother use to buy food?

A   **Mum-ney**   Paul R. aged 7

Q   What's a mother's favourite day of the week?

A   **Mumday**   Amelia T. aged 5

Q   What's a mother's favourite fruit?

A   **A bamama**   Sophie S. aged 5

Whacky Wally

For clever conversation
Talk to Pretty Polly
But if you want a giggle
Just watch Whacky Wally

Q   What do you call a wally in a clothes drier?

A   **A whirly**   Ian M. aged 7

Q   What do you call a wally on the wing of a jet?

A   **A windy**   Katie S. aged 9

Q   How do you get a one-armed wally out of a tree?

A   **Wave to him**   Pia K. aged 9

Q   Where do wallies go for holidays?

A   **Wally World**   Nikki B. aged 7

Q   What do you get if you cross a clown, Sherlock
    Holmes and a wally?

A   **A jolly wally, by golly**   Gina S. aged 6

Q   What do you get if you cross a wally with a parrot?

A   **A polly wally**   Gabriel M. aged 8

Q   Why did the wally fall out of the tree?

A   **Because he was tied to a koala**   Helen V. aged 6

Eskimos-es

*Igloo gags
And a rub of noses
The North Pole houses
Eskimos-es!*

Q What's an Eskimo's favourite car?

A An Eskimoke Con V. aged 9

Q What do Eskimos do before they kiss?

A They ug Anna S. aged 6

Q How do you keep an Eskimo cold?

A Take away the "mo" Aimee I. aged 7

Q What do you call an Eskimo that asks questions?

A An Askimo James T. aged 10

Q How do Eskimos hold their homes together?

A Ig-glue Louisa M. aged 8

Q   What do old Eskimos eat?

A   **Seals on Wheels**   Karly S. aged 6

Q   What do Eskimos wear on their heads?

A   **Polar hair**   James L. aged 7

Q   How do you know when two Eskimos are in love?

A   **They get nosy**   Josephine M. aged 9

Q   What falls at the North Pole but never gets hurt?

A   **Snowflakes**   Talia M. aged 7

Q   How do Eskimos transport snails?

A   **Es-cargo**   Georgia V. aged 9

Aussie Knock Knocks

Emus and koalas
Oceans and rocks
A joke book's not fair dinkum
Without Aussie Knock Knocks

Knock Knock

Who's there?

Cargo

Cargo who?

Cargo beep beep

Thomas L. aged 6

Knock Knock

Who's there?

Alison

Alison who?

Alison to the radio

Thomas L. aged 6

Knock Knock

Who's there?

Mister

Mister who?

Mister last train home

Billy M. aged 7

Knock Knock

Who's there?

My panther

My panther who?

My panther falling down   Marny S. aged 8

Knock Knock

Who's there?

Ammonia

Ammonia who?

Ammonia little boy   Lisa K. aged 7

Knock Knock

Who's there?

Vegemite

Vegemite who?

Vegemite not taste so good   Diana P. aged 7

Knock Knock

Who's there?

Saul

Saul who?

It's Saul over   Peter T. aged 8

Knock Knock

Who's there?

Romeo

Romeo who?

Rome-over to the other side of the lake   Peter T. aged 8

Knock Knock

Who's there?

Bed

Bed who?

Bedder late than never

Danielle M. aged 7

Knock Knock

Who's there?

Wombats

Wombats who?

Wombat's better than none

Brenda V. aged 9

Knock Knock

Who's there?

Dingo

Dingo who?

Dingo anywhere on the weekend

Thomas C. aged 7

Knock Knock

Who's there?

Emu

Emu who?

Emu all along

Bradley S. aged 8

Knock Knock

Who's there?

Caterpillar

Caterpillar who?

Cat-er-pillar of feline society

Mark L. aged 10

Knock Knock

Who's there?

Outback

Outback who?

Out back you'll find a rock

Guy S. aged 8

Knock Knock

Who's there

Kanaroo

Kanaroo who?

Kanaroo jump a six-foot fence?

Charlotte F. aged 9

Knock Knock

Who's there?

Koala

Koala who?

Koala Lumpur is not in Australia

Daisy F. aged 10

Knock Knock

Who's there?

Dubbo

Dubbo who?

Dub-bo fires the arrow
Alexis P. aged 7

Knock Knock

Who's there?

Adelaide

Adelaide who?

Adel-laide the snags on the barbie
Samantha T. aged 9

Knock Knock

Who's there?

Canberra

Canberra who?

Can-berra lot more than you think
Michelle T. aged 9

Knock Knock

Who's there?

Barbecue

Barbecue who?

**Barbecue for the
pool table, please**
Liam D. aged 10

Knock Knock

Who's there?

Footy

Footy who?

Foo-ty I'd like fish fingers please

Kym R. aged 9

Knock Knock

Who's there?

Cossie

Cossie who?

Cos-sie I'm a little confused by this

Georgia E. aged 9

Knock Knock

Who's there?

Coogee

Coogee who?

Coogee coogee coo

Kayla F. aged 7

Knock Knock

Who's there?

Yabbie

Yabbie who?

Ya-bbie a crayfish, man

Michelle F. aged 7

Flower Power

Wattles and waratahs
And gladioli tower
A rainbow of colour
It's Flower Power

Q   How do you recognise a flower in a speedway?

A   They put the petal to the metal   Joshua S. aged 7

Q   What kind of flower shows off all the time?

A   A posy   Eric B. aged 8

Q   Where do flowers go on holidays?

A   Gardenia   Oliver C. aged 6

Q   Why did the ivy cry?

A   Cause it weed   Harriet T. aged 9

295

Q   What do you call a strange plant?

A   **A weed-o**   Andrew F. aged 8

Q   What do you call an old flower?

A   **Poppy**   Max E. aged 7

Q   What do you call a stupid flower?

A   **A daffy-dill**   Kayleigh C. aged 7

Q   What type of tree can sit in your hand?

A   **A palm tree**   Hannah L. aged 6

Q   What do you call a flower that bites its lip?

A   **A tulip**   Angela S. aged 9

Q   What do you call a tree you can't find?

A   **A mys-tree**   Sonia R. aged 8

Thundering Underwear

Bloomers and boxers
Undergarments with flair
There is nothing as silly
As Thundering Underwear

Q What type of undies do scarecrows wear?
A **Wicker knickers**   Nicholas F. aged 7

Q What kind of underwear do bees wear?
A **Underbear**   Tyson P. aged 9

Q What type of undies do teachers wear?
A **Und-Ds**   Christian J. aged 8

Q What type of underwear packs a punch?
A **Boxer shorts**   Tina W. aged 9

Q What never sleeps and constantly needs changing?
A **A nappy**   Stan D. aged 9

Q   What do baby crabs wear?

A   **Nippy nappies**   Zoe Y. aged 8

Q   What did one pair of underpants say to the other?

A   **I need a change**   Kimberley R. aged 9

Q   What is a musician's favourite undergarment?

A   **A G-string**   Laura P. aged 9

Q   What is the best day of the week to change your
     underwear?

A   **Mundie**   Kenneth C. aged 7

Outback 'n' Beyond

There's roos and wombats
And a cane toad in a pond
There's a Budgee from Mudgee
Outback 'n' Beyond

Q What do you call 50 kangaroos running across the Harbour Bridge?

A **An illusion**   Emily F. aged 7

Q What kind of bat can't fly?

A **A wombat**   Catherine S. aged 9

Q What do you call a kangaroo that lives in Nimbin?

A **A hoppy hippy**   Carmel B. aged 7

Wow!... Heavy, man.

Q   What do you get if you cross a kangaroo and a cow?

A   **A kanga-moo**   Steven P. aged 7

Q   What do you get if you cross a kangaroo with a farmer?

A   **A jackaroo**   Brian W. aged 9

Q   When does an emu become a sheep?

A   **When you remove the "em"**   David L. aged 8

Q   What was the first Australian musical instrument?

A   **A ridgy didge**   Kylie B. aged 9

Q   What do you call a bird from Mudgee?

A   **A budgee**   Paul L. aged 6

Q   What did the cane toad say when he saw a bunny run by?

A   **Rabbit, rabbit**
Angus N. aged 7

Q   What's a kangaroo's favourite music?

A   **Hip hop**
Oscar C. aged 9

Chocolate Treats

It's the fabulous flavour
That nothing beats
We love to eat 'em
Chocolate Treats

Q What's an astronaut's favourite food?

A **A Mars Bar** Thomas L. aged 8

Q What's white and brown and goes to the movies?

A **A choc top** Robert F. aged 9

Q What type of chocolates live on rocks?

A **Oyster eggs** Gabrielle D. aged 7

Q What did the chocolate say to the lollipop?

A **See you later sucker**   Adrian L. aged 8

Q How do you stop someone eating your last chocolate?

A **Eat it first**   Blair P. aged 8

Preposterous Pets

No matter how silly
Your dog or cat gets
It couldn't compare to
These Preposterous Pets

Q What type of animal eats crumbs?

A **A crum-pet**
Hank M. aged 9

Q How do you start an animal race?

A **Ready, pet-ty, go**
Joshua C. aged 7

Q What type of animal eats cars and covers your floor?

A **A car-pet**
Rory T. aged 6

Q What do you call a bunch of protesting animals?

A **A pet-ition**
Kit F. aged 9

Q   What do you call an animal that whinges about small things?

A   **Pet-ty**

Jackson C. aged 6